CAMPAIGN SEASON

GLIMMER VALE CHRONICLES #6

MICHAEL KINGSWOOD

CONTENTS

ABOUT THIS BOOK

As Lydelton prepares for its regularly scheduled Mayoral election, long-simmering divisions within Glimmer Vale rear their heads. With his partner still out of town on a mission, it falls to Constable Raedrick Baletier to keep the peace, and get to the bottom of the brewing trouble.

But some resentments burn deep, and not everyone is looking for a peaceful settlement.

Campaign Season is the sixth book of the Glimmer Vale Chronicles, a political mystery set in a world of valor and magic.

Enjoy the book!

After you're done, please come to Michael's website and sign up for his mailing list at www.michaelkingswood.com/newsletter-signup/. Guaranteed to be spam free, he uses it to announce new releases and special promotions for his fans.

MAP OF GLIMMER VALE

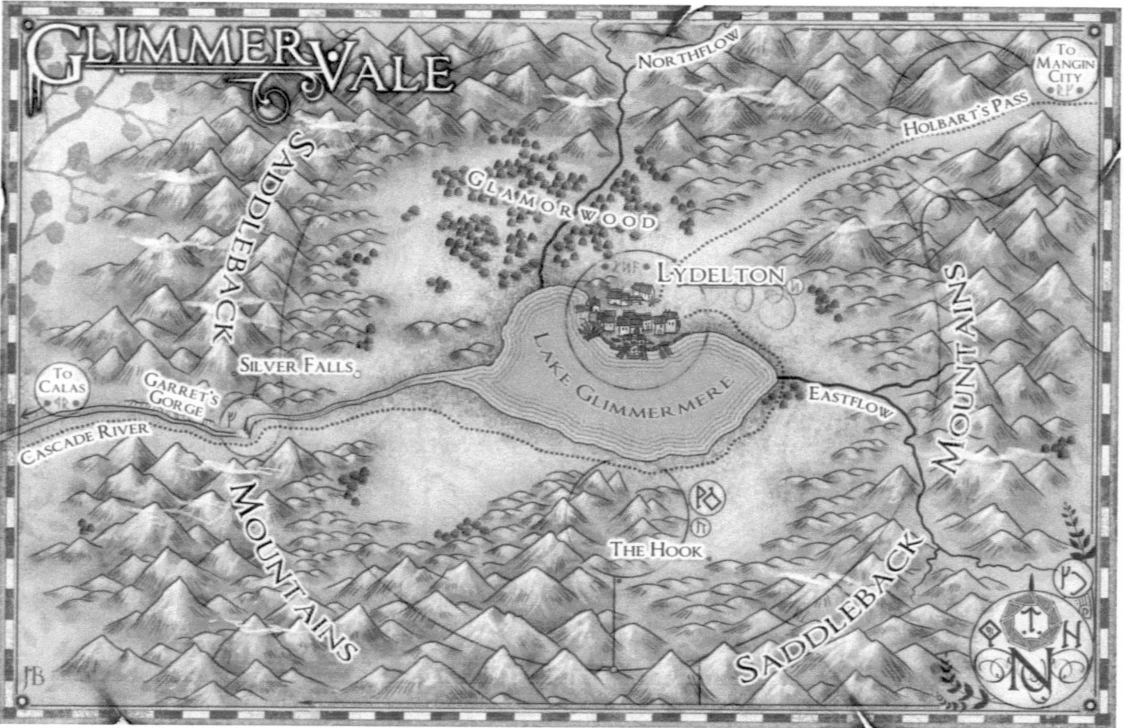
GLIMMER VALE
NORTHFLOW
To MANGIN CITY
HOLBART'S PASS
GLAMORWOOD
SADDLEBACK
LYDELTON
MOUNTAINS
Silver Falls
To CALAS
GARRET'S GORGE
Lake Glimmermere
EASTFLOW
CASCADE RIVER
MOUNTAINS
THE HOOK
SADDLEBACK
N

CAMPAIGNS

The crowd milling about in front of Lydelton's Town Hall was larger than any Raedrick had seen gathered in one place since he'd first come to Glimmer Vale a year and a half ago. Larger and, for a wonder, far better behaved than he would have expected, considering how many of them were fishing men--not well known for their docile behavior--and woodsmen or yeoman farmers from beyond the town's constructed limits.

Many faces were there amongst the several-hundred strong group of people that Raedrick had never seen before. Inwardly, that fact shamed him.

He, and his friend and long-time comrade-in-arms Julian, had become Constables of Lydelton, and by extension the rest of Glimmer Vale, shortly after they arrived in town. But Raedrick had only made a very few trips to visit the outlying farms and homesteads that dotted the valley beyond Lydelton's limits.

There simply hadn't been time, busy as his duties had kept him. And then after Lani became pregnant...

He shook his head. All of the people of Glimmer Vale were his charges, and though no one had done a proper census in years it was generally accepted that about the same number of people lived outside town limits as inside. And those numbered about a thousand adults.

"Should have made the time," he said under his breath.

There was no help for it now, of course. He'd just have to make a point of righting that error going forward.

But not today. No way he'd even think about leaving town today.

He turned his eyes from the milling crowd, toward the steps leading into the two-story Town Hall building itself. Or rather, toward the railed wooden stage that had been constructed in front of them. The wood was pine, no doubt harvested from the Glamorwood north and west of town, and for a wonder someone had gone to the effort to stain it into a dark, almost reddish brown. Buntings showing the Kingdom's colors--yellow and red and white--hung from the front of the stage's railing, and a single lectern had been set in place at the center of the stage. Also carved from pine, Raedrick recognized it from Mayor Brimly's office on the Town Hall's second floor.

The Mayor hadn't had cause to use it much, but today the lectern also was decorated, with the Kingdom's flag instead of just its colors.

A line of five chairs sat on the stage behind the lectern, four of them occupied by three people Raedrick recognized and one he did not; must be someone from an outlying farm. Mayor Brimly, plump and grey-haired, with bushy eyebrows and mustache, and a golden emblem of a fish jumping from the water of nearby Lake Glimmermere--the Mayor's badge of office--on the left breast of his dark blue jacket, was just ascending the ramp from the base of the Town Hall's stairs to the stage itself.

He looked rosy-cheeked, almost like he had run a mile to get there. But Raedrick knew that was not so; exercise was not the Mayor's strong suit.

No, more likely some of the many small but troublesome difficulties that the Mayor always had to deal with had him in a mood. Brimly never had been one to handle stress well. And then add his extra padding to the lingering heat of summer that continued on despite the calendar saying they were getting into autumn...

Everyone else on the stage was in his shirtsleeves, as were the vast majority in the crowd, and Raedrick himself. But Mayor Brimly always had to put on the best of appearances.

It wasn't that the Mayor was vain, per say. And Raedrick had to admit he had a point. The office of Mayor was the titular leader of the entire Vale, and that demanded the Mayor exhibit himself with a certain dignity and decorum. And people did respond more deferentially to a man who dressed well than one who did not.

Still, the Mayor was paying for that insistence on appearances now. Clearly visible sweat on his brow and the deep ruddiness of his cheeks said it all: he was not enjoying the day, and it didn't look to improve any time soon. The sun was lowering toward the mountain peaks to the east, but the day's heat showed no sign of letting up any time soon.

Raedrick suppressed a chuckle, and shook his head. That's the price you pay.

The Mayor stopped to clasp hands with the other four people in the chairs, then he stepped forward to the lectern and drew a breath, placing his hands down atop it.

The crowd, which had been a churning mumble of dozens of different conversations, quieted as he did so, and Mayor Brimly nodded greeting to them.

"People of Lydelton," he said with a gracious smile that seemed to take in every face in the crowd. He turned his head slowly, looking at them, and when his eyes met Raedrick where he stood off at the fringes of the group, it felt for a second like the Mayor was singling him out personally.

"It has been my greatest honor serving as your mayor these last three years," Mayor Brimly continued. "I've tried to be fair and just, and keep us pointed on a path of greater peace and prosperity for all."

A low murmur flowed through the crowd. It sounded like more people agreed with the Mayor's statement than didn't. But not by a whole lot.

Raedrick found his eyebrows lifting at that. He had certainly had his quarrels with the Mayor over the last year and a half. Mostly when the Mayor was being excessively timid, to Raedrick's thinking. But he had turned out to be right more often than he was wrong, and he certainly had worked tirelessly for the good of the town.

Raedrick had to concede, though, that he had much greater visibility into the Mayor's day to day dealings than most in town, and especially those who lived outside of town. So maybe he was missing something.

Mayor Brimly continued, "Nevertheless, my term ends in two months, and it is time to pick a new Mayor. Seated behind me are four who are standing for election. Pat Holcomb, from the fishing guild."

The man seated furthest to the left stood and raised his hand in a brisk wave. He was younger than the Mayor by ten or fifteen years, though completely bald. He had a lean, muscular look, and his clothing was plain but well-made: a white collared shirt that he wore with the sleeves rolled halfway up to his elbows and loose-fitting brown pants tucked into calf-high boots. It was hot for the grey cloak all the fishing men wore, but he had it draped over the chair behind him, to display his affiliation plainly.

"Brice Melton, owner of the Melton Ranch." The man to Holcomb's left stood and waved. He was more plump, and older than Holcomb by a few years, with black hair that was starting to go grey around the temple. He wore baggy grey pants and a dark blue shirt, and there was an emblem of some sort-- Raedrick was too far away to make out exactly what it was-- stitched into the right breast of his shirt. Around his neck he wore a leather band with a silvery charm or pendant that hung tightly between where his collar bones met. It flashed quickly in the sunlight as he moved, and he grinned broadly.

Raedrick didn't know him, except by name. His ranch was down by the Hook, a spur of peaks from the Saddleback Mountains that poked into the Vale on the southern side of Lake Glimmermere, forming a Vale with a Vale of sorts.

Raedrick had never visited it, but the ranch was supposed to be quite prosperous from word around town. As far as he knew, this was only the second or third time Brice had come into town since Raedrick and Julian first arrived.

Seemed strange he would want to run for Mayor, from that. But that was his business, not Raedrick's.

"Stepan Holiman," Mayor Brimly continued, gesturing toward the next man in the line of candidates. He was shorter than both the first two, but powerfully built. His face was round and though Raedrick couldn't see it he knew the man bore a number of burn scars on his cheeks, from embers or sparks that had flown up from his smithy's forge over many years of practicing his trade.

Stepan was dressed plainly, but his tunic and leggings were of good quality, and cleaned and pressed for the occasion. The laces of his tunic were undone halfway down his chest, a compensation for the heat, showing black chair on his chest that matched the flowing locks atop his head. They fell past his shoulders, giving him a more flamboyant look that Raedrick had seen from others in his trade.

Not for the first time, Raedrick wondered at the safety of hair that length around a forge. But Stepan hadn't had any issues that Raedrick had heard of. So far.

The blacksmith didn't wave when the Mayor pointed him out. Just stood, gave a serious nod, then seated himself once more.

Finally, Mayor Brimly pointed out the final man, slight of build but the tallest of the bunch, whose blue shirt no doubt set off the tone of his eyes quite well. His reddish hair was cut short on the sides and back, but was longer on top, hanging to just above his eyebrows, and he had a boyish face the belied his nearly forty years.

Tim Federson worked in a canvas shop, helping repair the sails and rigging of the fishing men's boats during the fishing season. But everyone in town knew him for his skill on the lyre and his singing voice, which often graced the common room of The Oarlock, and occasionally even the patio at Holb's Tavern, and earned him some pretty good tips from what Raedrick heard.

As well as the favor of more than one lass from around the Vale.

He had a bit of a reputation, and frankly Raedrick was surprised to see him amongst the candidates. But when the Mayor gestured his way and he stood and waved, a goodly number of people in the crowd near Raedrick voiced low-pitched approval at his presence up there.

Mayor Brimly paused and looked away from the candidates and back to the crowd. Then he took a deep breath, and the smile he had been wearing broke for a moment. "I regret to say that I will not be standing for re-election."

Little murmured conversations that had started up here and

there in the crowd as the other candidates had been introduced halted abruptly, a shocked silence sweeping over the crowd.

Not everyone liked the Mayor or the job he had done. But no one had expected him to not seek another term.

Certainly Raedrick had not. Mayor Brimly hadn't even hinted to him during their weekly meetings that he was leaning this way. If anything, he had appeared eager to get the election season going.

"Over the course of the next week, each candidate will have an evening to present his positions, and address questions you may have for him. Pat will begin this evening, followed by Brice, Stepan, and Tim. Then we will have a group forum where they will field your questions and compare and contrast their views with the other candidates."

Mayor Brimly paused for a breath. "The election will be one week from tonight. Please take the time to get to know each of these men, so you can make a good decision."

With that, the Mayor turned and descended the stairs, leaving the crowd, and from the expressions on their faces the other candidates as well, in surprised silence for a moment.

Then the discussions began in earnest.

2

INTRODUCTIONS

The discussions continued as the other three candidates who would not have the stage this evening followed the mayor and Pat readied himself for his presentation. He had a small wooden box tucked underneath his chair, which he stooped to retrieve, then he moved over to the podium and began arranging several documents that he took from it.

His speech, no doubt.

As Pat prepared, bits of nearby conversation washed over Raedrick. He picked out a mixture of disbelief that Brimly would not be running, some relief that he would not be, some sadness of that fact, but more than anything else curiosity as to why.

Raedrick shared that thought. Mayor Brimly clearly loved his position. From the first time Raedrick and Julian met him, he had seemed to puff up every time he had to take on an official duty; but not necessarily in a bad way. And Raedrick knew well how much Brimly cared for the population of the Vale. Though he didn't always agree with the way the Mayor chose to show it.

Brimly had retired from a very successful business running one of the few merchant caravans that passed through the

Saddleback Mountains between Mangin City and Calas, which were some of Lydelton's only connections and means of trade to the other areas of the Kingdom. And Raedrick was pretty sure he had retired in order to become Mayor.

A lot to leave behind to serve his people. And now to not even ask for another term?

It was a stressful job, to be sure. But Brimly surely enjoyed it. So what -

"A moment if you would, Constable?"

The baritone voice interrupted Raedrick's musings, and he turned to the left, facing the speaker.

And found himself looking eye to eye with Brice Melton.

The ranch owner wore an affable grin, but his eyes were shrewd as they met Raedrick's, and he immediately got an idea why Brice had been so successful. There was deep intelligence in those brown orbs, and he felt certain Brice had already sized him up and come to a pretty decent idea of his mettle.

This close, Raedrick could see that the emblem on his shirt was a capital M with a circle around it, stitched in silver. The pendant he wore was the same. The brand of his ranch, no doubt.

"Master Melton," Raedrick said, and extended his hand. "What can I do for you?"

The rancher clasped hands, and his grip was like a vice, belying the plumpness around his belly.

"It occurred to me that we've never actually met. I thought I ought to change that, all things considered."

Raedrick cleared his throat and put on an apologetic smile that was not at all feigned. "Yes, well, I should have stopped by your ranch. No excuse for that, but it has been - "

"- a remarkably busy year," Brice finished for him. He nodded gravely. "You don't have to tell me. We were doing alright holding off Farzal's bandits from my ranch before you and your partner showed up. But I doubt we could have held out too much longer had you not." He raised an eyebrow. "Word's reached us about the other things you've been up to since, and you ask me that's enough for ten years, not eighteen months."

His grin broadened, but his gaze remained just as level and appraising as it had been as he spoke. "And now your wife's just about due? No need to apologize. But I hope we will get more attention from you in the future, down in the Hook." His other eyebrow rose as he said that last.

"Certainly. Have there been problems? No word reached me or I would have - "

Brice waved a dismissive hand. "No, not really. But the hands could stand a reminder every so often that there is law around here beyond just my say so."

Raedrick crooked an eyebrow at him, and Brice let out a little chuckle.

"Nothing serious, Constable, I assure you. Nothing that a little chastisement couldn't handle. Still," he drew up slightly, "can't hurt to have the law around from time to time."

Raedrick felt himself beginning to frown. What exactly did Brice consider to be "a little chastisement?" But before he could give voice to the thought, the rancher continued on.

"There is another matter I'd like to discuss with you," he said, and glanced over toward the stage and the lectern.

Raedrick followed his glance and saw that Pat was settled in, his documents in whatever order he needed them. The fishing man stepped more close to the lectern and raised his hand, clearing his throat in a manner that somehow managed to carry over the various conversations within the milling crowd.

Those conversations slowly ceased, and a wave of turning heads and bodies flowed over the crowd as the assembled people gave Pat their attention.

Brice chuckled softly. "But that can wait until we have a more private moment. Good day, Constable." With that, he made a nod in Raedrick's direction and turned to go.

"Aren't you going to stay and hear what your competitor has to say?"

Brice stopped and looked back, an amused half-grin appearing on his face. "No need."

Then he walked away, his booted feet making soft but solid thumps on the flagstone paving of Lydelton's Main Street. Nearby members of the crowd parted to let him pass, then closed behind him and he vanished from sight.

"Well then," Pat said, drawing Raedrick's attention back to him. "I suppose you all want to know why I should be mayor."

A chorus of chuckles, mostly from other men of the fishing guild, swept through the crowd for a moment. Then the candidate commenced his speech.

3

———

DINNER GUESTS

he Oarlock was less crowded than usual. Only three of the tables spaced out around the common room were occupied, and at the bar that dominated the right-hand side of the room as one enters from outside sat only a single young man down near the end by the swinging doors that led back into the Inn's kitchens. A fishing man by his stature and the grey cloak they all wore, he mused over his tankard as though the contents contained the secrets to all of life, his stringy auburn hair obscuring his face from view.

The great flagstone fireplaces in the right and left corners of the room near the entrance were dark, a testimony to the lingering end-of-summer warmth even as night was closing in on the Vale. Oil lamps in brass sconces on the walls provided an intimate light, and the scents of spiced fish stew seeping in from the kitchens made Raedrick's mouth water.

Molly Millens, the Inn's slightly plump proprietress, was behind the bar, clad in a plain blue dress with her signature pristine white apron overtop, her greying hair pulled up into a bun on the top of her head. Rolf, the very caricature of a barkeep with a belly that overhung his pants but shoulders that spoke of heavy labor in his younger days, was wiping down the brass taps of the kegs stacked behind the bar with a rag that looked as though it had never seen a speck of dirt before in its existence.

Nevertheless, as Raedrick approached the bar, Molly said, "You missed a spot," to him, and pointed an imperious finger at the tap that Rolf had just been ministering to.

The light tone, and the jolly grin she flashed at him, took what sting there might have been out of her words, and Rolf grinned back, made an exaggerated half-bow, and moved back to the first tap.

Same old story with those two.

Raedrick slid onto a stool halfway down from where the lone fishing man sat, and immediately Molly's attention shifted from chivying her help. "Good evening, Raedrick," she said as she moved around Rolf to come a bit closer. "You're a little early. Dinner's not quite ready yet." She glanced back at the kitchen and raised a meaningful eyebrow.

It certainly smelled ready to Raedrick's nose, but he had long since learned not to question Molly's judgment when it came to the art of the kitchen.

On the other hand...

"Tell me you haven't been working Lani too hard."

Molly snorted softly. "She's not ready to pop just yet. No harm in her helping her elderly mother with her business until she does." Her eyes twinkled in the lamplight, and her smile turned ever so slightly impish.

Raedrick returned the snort. Elderly indeed. But a woman's age was another topic he had learned long ago not to approach.

Instead he glanced down the bar toward the lone fishing man. "Is Lester alright?"

Molly followed his glance and the little smile faded. "Not

sure. He came in right about an hour ago and hasn't budged. Not said a word either." She paused, and the corners of her mouth dipped. "Pretty sure that's his first drink."

Raedrick blinked. Fishing men weren't exactly known for their temperance, though Horace, the Guildmaster, made sure they didn't cause too much trouble. Still, Lester had spent a few nights in one of the holding cells in the back of the Constabulary after imbibing a bit more than was wise. It wasn't like him not to even finish one drink in an hour.

Raedrick felt his lips dipping to match Molly's, and he stood from his stool. Giving Molly a nod, he eased his way down toward where the young man sat, alone.

Lester noted his coming, as he turned to look up at Raedrick when he stopped by his side. "Constable," Lester said by way of greeting. His voice was a gravelly alto, not matching the otherwise youthful features of his round face. Only the tiniest of wrinkles at the corners of his hazel eyes pointed to days on end squinting in the sun out on Lake Glimmermere. And his mustache looked like it was struggling just to sit on his upper lip.

Raedrick wouldn't have bothered with it. But then he had never bothered with facial hair at all, until a bandit's cut had left him a scar on his chin.

He had to restrain himself from reaching up to rub at the black goatee that he now wore habitually, both to conceal the scar and because Lani thought it looked dashing.

A brief flash of heat ran through him as he recalled her expression when she'd first seen it on him, after a few days up in the mountains to check on the status of the project to rebuild Povol's hunting lodge, which the bandits in question had burned down.

Her reaction was...satisfying.

"Lester," Raedrick said, nodding in greeting. "How are things?"

Lester gave a little shrug and looked back down into his tankard. Up close, Raedrick could see that not only had he not finished it, it looked like he hadn't even taken a single drink.

"Not looking for company."

Raedrick nodded again, more slowly. "Are you - ?"

"I'm not causing any trouble, Constable. Minding my own business and just want to be left alone." Lester looked back at him and there was a fierce, confrontational light in his eyes. "Ok?"

Raedrick raised his hands, palms out in a calming gesture. "Ok, no worries. I'll leave you to it."

He took a step backwards, away from the young man, and Lester sniffed ever so slightly, then returned to staring into his tankard.

Raedrick paused, torn for a moment. There was definitely something wrong, but it wasn't like he and Lester were close, or even friendly. Their interactions had always been professional, and Lester wasn't making trouble, so why should the Constable be bothering him?

Molly's frown when he returned to his original spot spoke volumes, but she didn't say anything. Just met his eyes and gave a little, "Hey what can you do," kind of shrug and slid a tankard across the bar top toward him.

Rolf had apparently filled it, or maybe she had, while he was with Lester, and it was warm to the touch. Subtle spice lay over the fruity aromas that wafted from the tankard's top, carried on just a hint of steam. Mulled wine. Always delicious, and Raedrick couldn't help but smile in appreciation, even as his mouth began to water.

The first sip held up to the promise the scents had made, and the warmth of the fluid as he swallowed left a glow in his belly that spread quickly. Even in the relative warmth of the evening, that still felt good.

"Well," Molly said, nodding approval at his reaction to the drink, "I'll go get Lani hurrying up with supper." She raised an eyebrow, then scurried off before Raedrick could raise an objection. Lani was not in any condition to be hurried up about anything.

But a moment later, faster than Raedrick would have thought she could move if he hadn't known her as long as he had, Molli was gone through the swinging doors to the kitchen.

He couldn't help but chuckle.

A number of voices, boisterous and jolly, pulled Raedrick's attention toward the front of the common room, where a group of men, all clad in the fishing men's grey cloaks, were streaming in from the deepening night. There were about a dozen of the men, all talking overtop each other so the thread of their discussion was impossible to make out as they flowed en masse toward the bar. But the man in the middle of the group, who was receiving most of the group's attention, was plain to see: Pat.

Not unexpected, and it was clear that the fishing man turned mayoral candidate had his coworkers' support.

Also not unexpected.

The group took up station at the end of the bar closest to the entrance, opposite from where Lester was sitting, and formed a loose ring centered on Pat, who leaned back against the bar on his elbows and seemed to bask in the adulation of his fellows, a broad grin on his face as his people talked all around him.

One of the group broke off from the bunch, though, and meandered over toward Raedrick. Older than the rest, with grey hair and a thick grey beard that matched his cloak, and deep wrinkles on his face that came as much from the wind and rain out on the water as from the years.

Horace was head of the fishing guild, and had become fast

friends with Julian when he and Raedrick first came to town. Raedrick wasn't as close with him, but the old man had been more than helpful on many occasions since he and Julian had taken their positions as Constables.

"Constable," Horace said with a nod as he took the stool next to Raedrick's.

"Looks like Pat's speech went over with with your lot."

Horace sniffed and looked over at his people with amusement. "Course it did. He knows them well enough."

Raedrick raised an eyebrow, but held off from replying, instead taking another sip from his wine.

Silence lingered between him and the older fishing man for a moment, then Horace looked back at him. His lips twisted into a little smirk and he made a quick shrug of his shoulders. "Not sure how well it'll go with the rest of the town though."

Horace opened his mouth to continue, but his eyes flicked past Raedrick's face toward the end of the bar and the lone young fishing man sitting there. Immediately, any hint of amusement left Horace's face as his lips compressed into a tight scowl. "Crap."

Blinking, Raedrick lowered his tankard and set it back atop the bar, and turned to follow Horace's gaze toward Lester. "You know what's going on with - ?"

He stopped when he saw the younger man, who was now not just sitting and moping. He was rigid, upright, and staring daggers down the bar. But not toward himself, and not toward Horace, Raedrick was sure.

He panned back the other way, and felt a little surge go up his spine as he realized that Lester's ire was directed solely at one person: Pat.

"Crap," he said, echoing Horace even as he saw, from the corner of his eye, Lester slide off his seat and begin stalking toward the group of his guild mates.

"I've got this, Constable," Horace said, leaving his stool and bounding toward the younger man with all the grace of a man who had spent decades on bobbing boats, in all manner of weather. And never mind that he had at least 40 years on Lester.

The younger man stopped as Horace approached, holding hands up in a placating gesture. But the scowl on Lester's face spoke volumes. "Get out of the way, Horace."

"Easy, Lester," Horace said, his tone soft, almost comforting but with an edge of steel to it. "Let's go over to Holb's. Get an ale there."

Lester wasn't looking at Horace, but straight at Pat. Raedrick glanced over and saw Pat was returning the gaze levelly, his expression neutral except for a little tightening around the eyes.

The two men kept their gazes locked on one another, and after a few seconds the other fishing men around Pat took notice. Their boisterous conversation slowed, then died, and the group watched the stare down, obvious concern and no small amount of confusion on their faces.

"Let it go, Lester," Horace said softly, and took a half-step closer to the younger man.

He laid a hand on Lester's shoulder, and Lester gave a little jerk. His eyes flicked Horace's way and he stiffened. For a second, Raedrick thought he might strike Horace.

But then Lester gave a little jerk of a nod, and let himself be turned away from the bar, and Pat's group.

The silence as the pair of men wove their way through the mostly-empty tables toward the common room's front door was heavy with tension. At the door, Lester looked back and met eyes with Pat once again, and it felt like a conflagration about to light off.

Then they were out the door.

The heavy clunk of the solid oak door contacting its frame seemed to echo throughout the common room. Then one of the fishing men surrounding Pat said something Raedrick couldn't quite make out and the entire group broke out into laughter.

Pat joined in for a moment, but his chuckle was more reserved, fading completely as he raised his tankard to his lips.

His eyes never left the door Horace and Lester had just passed through.

4

BREAKFAST

"What's going on with Lester and Pat?" Raedrick said.

He regretted saying it almost as soon as he did. Not for the question but for the tone he used; he placed more force behind the words that he meant to, or even realized he was going to until they came out.

Horace shrugged and leaned back in his chair, scratching at his beard with his left hand.

They were sitting in Raedrick and Julian's office in the Constabulary. Small, one-story, and a block off of Main Street's paving stones, it was always a bit of a chore to keep the wooden planks making up the building's floor clear of dirt from outside. Today it was raining, so it was mud instead. Glorious.

The office area at the front of the building was just big enough for his and Julian's desks, facing each other on opposite sides of the room. Raedrick's was on the right as one enters, and had a rack of half a dozen swords on the wall behind it. Julian's side had bows, and a nice little wood stove that was mounted in the corner.

Several times last winter, Raedrick had regretting not

claiming that desk when they had divvied up duties, and office territory. Raedrick had picked his because it provided a bit easier access to the barred door leading back to the line of holding cells in the rear of the building.

Leave it to Julian to see the benefits of comfort over functionality.

Next to the door to the holding cells was a bookcase filled with town and Kingdom ordnances, and records of the various cases he and Julian, and their predecessors, had worked. The bookcase, like the walls and floor--and the building in its entirety really--was unstained pine, cut from trees in the Glammorwood north of Lake Glimmermere.

Not large, but functional, and it met Raedrick's needs well enough. For the most part.

But right then, what he needed--well, maybe that was too strong a word. What he <u>wanted</u> was an explanation about the near-confrontation between the two men last night. Even if one of them wasn't a candidate for mayor, that looked like the sort of thing that needed to be put to bed quickly, before it became trouble.

A caravan had just left town last week, on its way from Calas to Mangin City, and the caravan's hands had caused enough trouble to keep Raedrick in paperwork the rest of the month. He really did not need more. Not with Lani ready to give birth any hour now, and no matter what Molli said.

Raedrick glanced over at the other desk in the room, its empty chair pushed neatly in and its dark blue blotter blessedly unburdened by papers. Not for the first time, he wondered how Julian and Melanie fared in their quest to take Jared Tolburt to The Falconer's Stairs. They had been gone several months, so they should be returning soon.

In fact, Raedrick would have expected them to have already returned, if all had gone well on their journey. What if -

He realized Horace was talking and snapped his attention back to the old fishing man. "Sorry?"

Horace stopped mid-word and raised an eyebrow at him, then glanced sidelong at Julian's desk as well for a second. "Any word from them?"

Raedrick shook his head. "I'm sure they are having an interesting time of it." He grinned. "You know Julian."

Horace snorted out a half-laugh, then turned back to meet Raedrick's gaze and that moment of amusement fled as quickly as it had come. "I was saying, I don't rightly know what's got their backs up but they got into a bit of a tussle on the boat during offload yesterday. Lester wouldn't tell me a thing last night, just that Pat has it coming."

Raedrick leaned back in his chair and worked hard to suppress a groan. That was all he needed--trouble in the middle of the campaign. "Horace, I can't have - "

Horace held up a hand and Raedrick stopped. "I've taken steps. Moved Lester to a different boat that moors at the opposite end of the finger piers from Pat's. And moved him to the evening shift. Most they'll see of each other is maybe a minute or so when Lester's heading home and Pat's coming in."

Raedrick frowned. "That leaves the rest of the day still."

A shrug preceded the words Raedrick knew Horace would say. "I can't control what they do on their own time. I'm not the Constable."

Raedrick just looked at him for a second. They older man looked right back, and Raedrick saw the resolve there but also knew Horace had the right of it. Though it certainly irked a bit. He sighed.

"Well they'll be on different sleep cycles too, so that will help. I'll just have to keep an eye on Lester the next few days. Or have Hiram or Gilroy do it."

And it was lucky that he had that option. Hiram and Gilroy

were two of the fishing men who had volunteered to stand with Julian and Raedrick when they first came to town and took on the brigands that had been harassing the Vale. Good men. With Julian gone, he had enlisted their help keeping the peace.

He wasn't sure how he would have dealt without their assistance these last few months, especially when the caravans came through.

Horace shook his head. "That's the other thing I wanted to talk to you about. We're into autumn now and we're a little off our target for the year's catch. Covington Brothers don't want us missing it, and neither do I. So I have to pull them back to the boats."

Raedrick couldn't suppress the groan that came out then. "You're kidding me. Horace, I've got - "

"There will be snow in the passes in a few weeks. There might be one more caravan before Spring. So not much chance of major trouble. But Hiram and Gilroy are two of my strongest backs. And if we don't meet our target..." Horace didn't complete the sentence. He didn't have to.

The Covington Brothers' fishing company was the largest business in the Vale. Fully a third of the men in town worked the boats, and a good percentage of the remaining industry supported them in one way or another. The brothers had sold the bulk of the summer catch to the last couple of caravans that came through. Now the catch was going into the town's winter food stores.

Miss the target, and it promised to be a lean winter, and not just from a profit perspective.

Raedrick nodded. It grated, but Horace was right. He could deal with a couple busy weeks.

And who knows, maybe Julian would show back up soon to take back some of the burden.

"Alright. But how about you put one of the two of them on Lester's boat. Either of them friendly with him?"

Horace's lips turned upward into a sly smile. "Done." He stood from his chair, stretching slowly as his body shifted. Raedrick for a second thought he could hear the old man's joint's popping, but if that caused Horace any discomfort he didn't show it. "I'd best get back to the docks," Horace said. "Got the morning offload to see to."

"Have fun with that."

Horace flashed a smile that said exactly how much he did just that. Then he turned, flipped the cowl of his grey cloak over his head, and stepped out into the sprinkling rain outside.

At least it wasn't the downpour it had been when Raedrick had tromped over from his and Lani's house, caddy corner to The Oarlock.

But right then, it felt like he was getting all the rain in the world dumped right on him.

He looked back over to the right, to the empty chair that should have held his friend's cheerful, but at times exasperating, form.

"Hurry up and get back here," he said into the empty room.

The slow drumming of raindrops on the roof overhead was the only answer.

5

RABBLE ROUSING

It didn't take very much discipline for Raedrick to push himself away from his desk, and the report that had taken up the majority of his morning, buckle on his sword-belt, throw the black cloak that Melanie had given him as a wedding present over his shoulders, and head out for his noon-time patrol of Lydelton's streets.

He had been itching to get away from the cussed paperwork for the last hour; sticking with it was the part that took effort.

The rainfall had faded to barely above a drizzle, and as he stepped outside a break in the clouds off to the east let a beam of sunlight shoot down onto the tip of one of the peaks in that portion of the Saddleback Mountains. The whiteness of the mountains' ever-present snowcaps seemed to almost flash in response to the beacon from the heavens, and Raedrick breathed deeply of the rain-cooled, moist air, feeling the weight fall from his shoulders like he had shed a heavy pack after a long day's walk.

Uphill.

He clumped down the stairs leading up to the Constabulary's front porch, then past the hitching posts out front toward

Main Street. At first he tried to avoid the biggest of the puddles in the muddy side street where his office lay, but after a few paces he stopped bothering; there was no avoiding the mud either way.

His pace improved one he got to Main Street's flagstones, and he set off west, toward Town Hall and the speaking platform that had been erected there for the campaign.

But when he was still a block away, he slowed, then stopped.

A small crowd had gathered in front of the grandstand: a loose circle of around a dozen men with the cowls of their cloaks drawn up over their heads. One of them, standing with his back to the grandstand, was speaking, and gesticulating with quick, forceful chops of his hand. From his movements, he appeared agitated, and that agitation seemed to be spreading through the group.

This didn't look good. At this hour most folks were taking to their noon meals or tending to chores, not gathering in public.

And certainly not getting riled up.

Raedrick continued toward the group, speeding up to a fast walk. The group's energy seemed to pick up with his every step until, when he finally got within earshot the tension was so tight he could have cut it with a butter knife.

The speaker wasn't helping.

" - show him that we're not going to take it anymore!" he said in a gravelly voice that carried entire levels of affront and outrage.

Raedrick recognized the voice, though the man's face was still obscured by his cowl from this angle. Jeb Tomason. One of the hands at the Henson farm, which lay a short ways outside the town proper, where the Eastflow met Lake Glimmermere.

Jeb lived in Bixby's Boarding House, and Raedrick and Julian had come calling there several times over the last year and a half over some trouble or other that Jeb had caused, or gotten caught up in somehow.

Figured he would be the center of this growing whatever-it-was.

"What's going on, gentlemen?" Raedrick said in his, "Listen up," tone of voice. The one he used for making battlefield orders, back in his Army days.

The group gave a collective jerk, like he had surprised the lot of them, and the men turned to regard him. Raedrick recognized most of the faces. All were men who helped families who owned farms in the environs around Lydelton keep and maintain their fields and livestock. Most had up until now been quiet, competent men who did their jobs, raised their families, and caused no trouble.

But all wore scowls on their faces.

And none more than Jeb. He fixed Raedrick with a glare and a clenched jaw that almost said he was ready to throw down right then and there.

That wasn't like him. He'd gotten into trouble, but it had never been serious; never anything that required more than a dressing down from Raedrick or Julian to get him back in line.

No one spoke for several seconds. They just looked at Raedrick bitterly, while Jeb seemed almost to be chewing on his tongue.

"Ok," Raedrick said, in as level and no-nonsense a tone as he could manage. The tone that had more than once made a Private spill the beans from fright, back in the day. "Out with it, Jeb."

The farmhand continued the glare for another second, but dropped his eyes once Raedrick focused fully on him. He didn't drop his scowl though, and when he spoke there was bitter anger in his voice.

"What's going on is those bastards down in the Hook are

trying to run us out of our jobs. That's what's going on, Constable!"

Raedrick blinked, Jeb's words making him pause for a moment. "What do you mean?"

"Melton means to take over all the other farms in the Vale! Shut them down, or move his own people in and keep the profits for himself!"

That came from one of the older men in the group, off to Raedrick's left. He was the only one with grey in his hair, and Raedrick didn't know his name offhand. But he'd seen him around, and he had never appeared to be given to flights of fancy before.

"What are you talking about? Who said that?"

Jeb thrust his chin out. "He's keeping it hush-hush, but I got word of it from a friend of a friend who works down on Melton's ranch. The hands are practically slaves down there, and that's what they mean to turn us into!"

A few mutters from other men in the small crowd told Raedrick there was general assent--or at least belief--in this sentiment.

He shook his head. "Men. You haven't even heard Brice's speech yet. You don't know what he's going to propose - "

"Don't matter what he says," said the grey-haired man again. "He's a thieving liar! Give him the power and he'll just do it!"

This was starting to get out of hand. "Ok, that's enough. Don't you men have work to do?" Raedrick fixed Jeb with a hard stare. "I know the Hensons' fence isn't mended yet."

Jeb seemed to deflate a bit. His shoulders sagged and the pugnacious frown faded. He coughed slightly and looked away, down Main Street in the direction of the Henson farm. "They said I could have the next couple days, on account of the election."

"Did they." Raedrick crossed his arms over his chest and put on a doubtful frown. "Well I bet they didn't mean for you to start playing rabble rouser." He looked back over the rest of the group, who suddenly seemed a bit less rambunctious as well. "Get out of here. Go make yourselves useful until Brice has his say tonight."

"He don't have nothing good to say," said grey hair, but a bit less forcefully than before.

"Then don't vote for him. But for now, get going." The group shuffled their feet, looking uncertain, but no one actually started to move. So he barked, "Now!" in his parade ground voice.

They went. Fast.

Jeb looked back at Raedrick as he hustled away down Main Street. It wasn't a friendly look. But at least he was going.

Raedrick watched them go, and shook his head. "Bloody wonderful," he said under his breath.

This was going to be a very tiring few days, looked like.

6
____

CONCERNS

ayor Brimly's office was on the second floor of Town Hall, up a darkly polish staircase that could easily take three men abreast. His door was heavy pine, stained dark like the stairs, and had a polished brass latch that was worn and smudged by years of hands pressing on it, and no matter how much the Mayor's assistant labored to keep it gleaming.

The door was open when Raedrick ascended from below, Brimly seated behind his great desk of office in his shirtsleeves, which he had rolled up to the elbows now that he was out of public view. His jacket, dark green today and as usual bearing the golden badge of his station, hung from a peg on the wall to the right of his desk, and he was bent over a sheaf of papers, squinting through reading glasses at the report.

The odor of pipe smoke filled the room, despite the great window behind the desk being cracked open. The ongoing drizzle had reduced the normal midday breeze to nearly noth-ing, and a wisp of residual smoke lifted from his pipe where it lay on an ashtray to his left next to his desk blotter, adding to the lingering smell.

Raedrick paused in the doorway and rapped quickly on the frame, and the Mayor's eyes lifted. He blinked upon seeing Raedrick and leaned back in his chair, which creaked softly at his motion.

Removing his reading glasses, Mayor Brimly said, "Constable. I don't believe we had a meeting this afternoon?"

Raedrick shook his head and stepped into the room. "I have a concern."

Brimly frowned slightly, then gestured toward one of the two simple wooden chairs that were laid out in front of his desk.

"When you have concerns, the town tends to be near the brink of destruction," he said in a light tone that carried just a smidgeon of worry.

Chuckling softly, Raedrick settled into the proffered chair and waved a dismissive hand. "Nothing that severe. I hope. But I've noticed a few things that we may want to get ahead of."

He took a minute to describe the incident with Lester and Pat, and the one with Jeb.

A few seconds of silence followed, then Brimly laughed.

Raedrick cocked an eyebrow at him, and the Mayor shook his head. "I sometimes forget how short a time you've been here. You haven't seen one of our elections before."

"I've seen them elsewhere."

"True." Brimly swiveled his chair halfway around--his was the only chair in town that could do that, and it was marvelous--and looked out the window toward Main Street below. "But you may have noticed people here can be stubborn."

That was an understatement. Raedrick nodded.

"It comes out in force during election season. Folks have their pet peeves, and decide this is the time to give them voice. The week will be full of debates and little arguments. But then they'll vote, the new Mayor will be sworn in, and all will go back to normal. Happens every time."

"That thing between Pat and Lester didn't seem to be just a difference of opinion."

Mayor Brimly nodded, and looked back at Raedrick with a cocked eyebrow. "What are you doing about it?"

"Horace got him moved to a different boat and I have some people watching to make sure nothing goes badly between them."

"Then it's covered."

"Yes, but - "

"I wouldn't worry about this thing with Brice either," Brimly said. "There's been tension between him and the smaller farmers for a while. They think he's trying to crowd them out of business. He thinks they're uppity and envious of his success." He shrugged. "There's a bit of truth to both. But if you ask me, he's the right man for the office, after I leave. He knows how to run an organization that goes beyond his nose."

After he leaves. So Brimly <u>was</u> set on going; it wasn't just an election-week ploy.

Brimly must have seen the thought on Raedrick's face, because he let out a little half-chuckle. "You won't be sad to see me go, Raedrick. Admit it."

"We don't always agree, that's true, but it's worked pretty well overall."

Brimly nodded, then looked back out the window. "I have my reasons. Just leave it at that." His eyes grew distant as he focused on something out in the distance, in the direction of the lake. After a moment, he added, "Truth be told, I'll be happy to be rid of the burden."

From the expression on his face, part wistful and part resigned, Raedrick wasn't so sure of that.

They sat in silence for a few moments more, Raedrick unsure how to respond to the Mayor's statement. Then Brimly gave himself a little shake and returned his full attention to

Raedrick. That pensive expression was gone, and he was all business, his eyes narrowed, focused.

"I don't think there is reason to be truly concerned. But keep an eye out." He paused, then added in a tone of command, "Keep me informed."

Raedrick nodded. "Of course."

Brimly returned the nod, then made a quick gesture toward the door. He re-donned his reading glasses, then scooted a bit closer to his desk and picked up the papers he had ben reading when Raedrick arrived.

Accepting the dismissal for what it was, Raedrick stood and moved quickly toward the open doorway.

Time to get back about his rounds.

7

PLANS AND DISRUPTIONS

*B*rice was dressed to the nines. Whereas yesterday he had been in shirtsleeves, this evening he had on a formal coat--black with silver trim with that same sigil stitched into the right breast--and stiffly-pressed leggings. His boots came to just below his knees, their black polished so that the lowering sun glinted off their toes as he stepped up to the campaign lectern. He wore the same silver pendant, and an affable grin that turned his face into the very picture of open cheeriness.

A far cry from Pat's casualness yesterday; Brice's every movement spoke of a man in command of himself and his surroundings.

The crowd was every bit as large as it had been yesterday; perhaps a bit larger, Raedrick thought as he looked around and did a quick estimate. Probably Brice had directed his hands to attend today, whereas he may not have enforced attendance yesterday, or for the next two days.

Pad the crowd with your supporters. Not a bad plan.

But Raedrick's thoughts jumped to Jeb's words of a few hours ago, and he wondered if the rumor Jeb heard about conditions at the Melton ranch was correct. If so, would Brice's people really support him?

They may have no choice.

Raedrick pushed that thought from his mind. He had never heard any reports of malfeasance from Melton, no complaints from any of the hands who had come up to town over the last year and a half. And if things were as bad as Brice's detractors said, he should have.

He flashed back to Brimly's explanation: just election season bickering and exaggeration.

Most likely correct.

The crowd hushed quickly as Brice raised his hands in greeting. But then he already had their attention from his appearance and his entrance.

"Good evening, friends," Brice began.

A few people replied with their own greetings from elsewhere in the crowd, which Brice acknowledged with an even bigger grin and a nod.

But off to Raedrick's left he heard one person snort. And another bitter-sounding mutter from in front of him somewhere.

Not all had fallen for Brice's charm yet. Surprising if they had, really.

"It is my honor to be here to ask for your vote. I have a vision of greater prosperity. Not just for my ranch," he added after someone off to the right made a snide-sounding comment that Raedrick couldn't quite make out but Brice clearly did. "No. And not just for the town of Lydelton. But for all of Glimmer Vale."

Brice paused, and held up a piece of paper, turning it toward the crowd. There was writing on it, but it was too far away for Raedrick to see.

"This is a record of caravan traffic through the Vale for the last fifteen years," Brice said.

Where did he get that? Raedrick didn't have that data. Maybe the Covington Brothers; they certainly would have business records of their dealings with the caravans coming through. Or the Mayor's office, since caravans had to register there. Still, he didn't think anyone had bothered to tabulate it before.

But clearly Brice had.

"We all know what happened after the Kingdom claimed and cleared the southern passes," Brice said, pointing at a point two thirds of the way down the page. "It went from an average of twenty caravans per year to half a dozen."

"Easier trip," said someone in front of Raedrick, and received murmured agreements from those around him.

"It's understandable. Our passes are difficult," Brice said, echoing the anonymous man's statement, "and the snows come early and melt late compared to those in the south. But it was a blow to this community. Since then our population has declined drastically as people moved away to Mangin City or other places further east. And we've all seen our incomes dwindle." Brice paused, put the paper down, then drew a breath. "I have a plan to change that. To draw business back to Glimmer Vale, and make our town into a growing and prosperous city. Not just a half-remembered smudge on the Kingdom's map."

Raedrick felt a surge run up his spine, a mixture of intrigue, excitement even, over the prospect that Brice claimed to be offering; but also of dread.

Part of the reason he and Julian had opted to remain in Glimmer Vale was because it was so isolated, so overlooked by the Kingdom at large. No one would know, or the ones who did would not care, about his and Julian's status as deserters from the Army.

Their secret was out to an extent. Marshall Leminster down in Mangin City had discovered the truth, but Raedrick and Julian had come to an arrangement with him: they kept the peace in the Vale and supported him when they could, and he kept his knowledge of their status to himself.

Mutually beneficial, but it only worked because Lydelton was unnoticed by the higher authorities. If Glimmer Vale rose to prominence, and attracted more official attention...

He swallowed. Hard. That surge in his spine turned into a chill.

Julian could move on, if he had to. But Raedrick had a wife here, and soon a child. He couldn't force them to leave their home, if -

He realized he had lost track of what Brice was saying, and pulled his thoughts back in order. Time enough to worry over that possible problem if it reared its head.

"Yes we can," Brice said, apparently in response to a voiced skepticism from the crowd. "If we - "

He was interrupted by a woman's frightened, almost terrified, scream from off to the left.

Raedrick spun in that direction and began pushing through the crowd, his right hand coming to rest on his sword hilt.

"Get the Healer's Circle!" Someone shouted from ahead.

"Constable!" Came another shout.

He wasn't moving fast enough. Bodies were blocking him; some moved easily at his touch, some resisted and pushed back.

"MOVE!" he roared, and a path parted before him, men anxiously getting out of his way and pulling companions who moved too slowly. Women pulling children to themselves, sudden fright on their faces.

And then he was through into the open, and saw the source of all the commotion.

A young man man with sandy hair in a fishing man's cloak, sprawled on his back on the flagstones of the street, clutching at a bloody gash across his abdomen.

Two other fishing men crouched next to him, trying to give

aid. But the spreading pool of blood, growing in a crimson circle around the fallen man, told Raedrick their help would be in vain. The cut had severed an artery, for certain. Even Master Sebastini, with all his skill, would be hard pressed to save the young man. And the Healer's Circle was several blocks away.

Raedrick slowed, that chill in his spine turning to ice like that on the summit of Tollard's Peak. He didn't need to fully see the victim's face to know who it was.

Lester.

8

TAKING STOCK

"This is completely unacceptable!"

Brice Melton's face was flushed, his features twisted into such a caricature of outrage that Raedrick would have thought someone had just insulted his mother while making a play for his wife. He loomed, despite not being of overly substantial height, and his words flowed toward Mayor Brimly like a flood.

For his part, Brimly stood firm against Melton's tirade, his feet planted solidly on the floor planks of his office and his arms crossed over his chest.

The Mayor's Office was full, almost to bursting, for this emergency council. Raedrick, the Mayor, and Melton, along with the other mayoral candidates--except Pat--Ravi Sebastini from the Healer's Circle, and Horace.

"A man is dead, Master Melton."

It was Sebastini who answered Brice's words. The elderly head of the Healer's Circle, slight of frame but powerful of mind, wore the yellow and white of his order. And though he spoke softly, his words whipped through the air with a vigor that denied the possibility of their not being heard.

Brice didn't even flinch. He looked sidelong at Sebastini and gave a quick nod of acknowledgement. "Indeed. And where is the killer, Constable?"

His affronted eyes came to rest fully on Raedrick. Perhaps he thought to intimidate him with his ire, but Raedrick had seen worse from harder men.

He shrugged. "We don't know who the killer is. When we - "

"Oh come on! It's obvious who did it: Holcomb. Everyone in town has heard about the trouble between those two. Where is he?"

"That's not obvious, actually. But I have people looking for him. He wasn't at your speech," if anything, Brice's cheeks went even more red at that--did he actually think Pat should have listened to him when he hadn't been willing to do the same for Pat yesterday?--"and he's not at home. Men are sweeping the town now, and they'll bring him in when they find him."

"Which men? His?" Brice pointed at Horace, who simply scowled in response.

Brice rolled his eyes and looked back at the Mayor. Taking a deep breath, he visibly drew himself together, then spoke again, his words more measured. "I have no doubt the Constable will get to the bottom of this matter and see justice done. But in the meantime I've been cheated out of the time allotted to me. How can there be a proper campaign if the candidates are not able to make their cases?"

Brimly cocked an eyebrow at him. Cheated, indeed. "What do you suggest, Brice?"

"Move the events a day to the right. I will finish my speech tomorrow, and then we proceed as before."

"The law requires the election next week," Sebastini said, in the same low tone of voice. "What you propose would deny the people time to think adequately about their choice."

"And denying me the right to finish presenting my proposal does the same!"

Brimly sighed and shook his head. "Calm down, Brice. No one's denying you anything. But Ravi is right; we are constrained by the law. And - "

"He can have some of my time tomorrow."

All eyes went to the speaker: Stepan, the blacksmith. His voice was higher pitched than his bulky frame and burn-scarred cheeks would have predicted. It always set Raedrick back a bit, no matter how many times he had interacted with the man.

"Are you sure, Stepan?" Brimly said. "All candidates are supposed to get equal time."

The smith shrugged. "I don't have all that much to say." He looked sidelong at Brice, then added, "And if it'll shut him up..." He shrugged again.

Horace barked out a laugh of amusement that he quickly suppressed. But the damage was done. Smirks appeared on Tim and Sebastini's faces, and Raedrick thought he saw a quick flash of a grin on the Mayor's face as well, but it vanished as quickly as it came as he looked gravely back at Brice.

"Will that be acceptable?"

Brice glowered at Stepan for a second, but then drew himself up and, sucking in a quick inhalation, he nodded Brimly's way.

"Then it is decided. We will convene as planned tomorrow. But Brice," the Mayor pointed a finger at him, "keep it brief. No theatrics. No lofty verbiage. Just spell out the rest of your proposal and step aside." His eyebrows rose. "Don't want to cheat Stepan out of his time, do we?"

"Of course not," Brice said, his words back to a more normal tone of voice. He glanced aside at the smith. "Wouldn't dream of it."

Brimly nodded. "Well then, I suppose we're done with you candidates for the evening. Thank you, gentlemen."

Stepan and Tim nodded and turned toward the door. Brice looked like he was about to object. But he evidently thought the better of it, and taking the dismissal he turned to follow his fellows.

When the door closed behind them, Brimly let out of long, exasperated sigh and turned his eyes toward the ceiling, like he was saying a quiet prayer to the gods for patience. At least, that's what Raedrick would have been doing in his place.

After a heartbeat, the Mayor looked back at him. "I have to say I'm in agreement with Brice, Constable. Pat seems the logical suspect to me. And I thought you said you had people watching to make sure this sort of thing didn't happen?"

"Pat didn't have a gripe with Lester. It was the other way around." Horace answered the Mayor before Raedrick could. Whatever amusement he had entertained from Stepan's quip was gone; his face was a serious mask, his tone grim. "Before you ask, I don't know why. Lester wouldn't say specifics and when I talked with Pat this morning, he was the same."

Brimly frowned. "Could be self defense then. Maybe Lester attacked him and Pat fought him off."

Sebastini said, "That is possible. The cut on Lester's abdomen was almost certainly made by a sword or long knife." Which didn't exclude Pat--the fishing men all kept blades for cleaning and scaling their catches, and for other uses aboard the boats. "One long, quick cut. The blade must have been very sharp, and wielded with skill." The Healer shook his head. "I'm amazed Lester was able to make it to the crowd without spilling his intestines everywhere."

The Mayor's frown deepened, and Raedrick didn't have to ask why.

Pat wasn't a trained fighting man, not with a sword anyway. Most of the townfolk were not. But almost everyone had a sword or an axe up in the attic somewhere. And it didn't take all that long to figure out how to swing one effectively if no one is trying to cut you at the same time.

So really the list of potential suspects was pretty large, if Pat wasn't their man.

"When we find Pat I'll get the details about his conflict with Lester," Raedrick said. "But at the moment I don't want to jump to any conclusions. From the blood trail, looks like Lester was attacked in the alley half a block down from Town Hall. But with all the mud from the rain, it's going to be hard to backtrack the attacker, what with all the other traffic that's goes through that section of town. So if it's not Pat..." He left the rest unsaid.

"Going be a hell of a task to solve it," the Mayor said for him. He drew himself up and sniffed in a quick breath. "Well that's why we have you, Constable. Do you need anything?"

Raedrick looked over at Horace. "Gilroy and Hiram?"

Horace frowned to match the Mayor. His eyes flicked between Brimly and Raedrick. "There's the catch target."

Brimly snorted. "What difference will two men make that the other two hundred aren't already doing? So a boat might have to stay out an extra day or two as the season closes to make the target. That's a small price to pay to clear up this matter."

"Easy enough to say from a nice warm office," Horace said, but there was no real challenge in his tone. He was clearly making the argument just to make it. From the look in his eyes he knew the right answer. "I'll talk to the Covington Brothers. With what's happened I think they'll go along."

"Well you tell them to come see me if they have a problem with it," the Mayor said. He looked around at the other men in the room. "Anything else?"

Head shakes all the way around, and Brimly nodded.

"Alright. Get to it, Constable. I want this cleared up before election day--or at least I want Pat cleared before then, so this doesn't affect his candidacy."

"If he's innocent," Raedrick said.

"Yes. If." From the look on Brimly's face, he didn't think that was likely, whatever reservations Raedrick may have expressed.

Inwardly, Raedrick agreed.

9

MANHUNT

*H*iram and Gilroy were both fishing men, but they were so dissimilar in stature that Raedrick sometimes had to force himself to remember they both followed the same trade--and were very skilled at it.

Hiram was shorter, thin, and moved with a natural grace that left no doubt as to his ability to remained balanced on a rocking boat. In fact, he was often the one who went aloft on the mast to fix issues with the boat's sail or rigging. He had quickly become skilled with the bow once Raedrick and Julian began teaching their volunteer army, and in the last six months he had been coming to Raedrick for lessons with the sword as well, and doing quite well at it.

He was mostly bald except for a small brown strip just above his ears that continued down around the back of his head, and his hazel eyes were set in a continual squint from years of sun glare on the water, but he wasn't un-handsome. His wife was comely, and they had six children between them.

Not bad work.

Gilroy, on the other hand, was almost as wide as he was tall, a mixture of muscle and fat that at first made Raedrick wonder over his fitness. That quickly proved not an issue; the man had the stamina of a bull, and the mop of hair and extravagant beard to go with it. His nose was broad and crooked, the leavings of one too many tavern brawls Raedrick assumed--though he hadn't gotten into any trouble since Raedrick and Julian had taken over.

In fact, Gilroy alone had defused more than a few near rows that one or another caravan crews had begun to start during their days in town.

But no one would accuse him of excessive grace; he looked more like a blacksmith that a man of the boats. All the same, he was one of the more highly regarded hands out on the water. A wizard with the nets, and no wonder from the girth of his arms.

Good men, and Raedrick was happy for their help. But right then neither of them looked at all pleased with themselves, and truth be told neither was Raedrick.

They were in what had been Lester's flat: a small, simple room, sparsely furnished with a cot in one corner, a three-drawer cabinet against the wall caddy-corner to it, and a stand for hanging cloaks and hats next to the door. A single window, open against the lingering warmth of the day, lay above the cabinet, facing east. Through it the last residuals of sunset, now just a whitish smudge above the dark peaks of the Saddleback Mountains, was barely visible.

The room was dimly lit by a single oil lamp adjacent to the door, and there were a pair of unlit candles in sconces on either side of the window.

The furniture was all well-crafted from local pine but unstained, and there wasn't much in the way of personal decoration up on the walls.

It was like Lester slept here, but didn't really live in the space.

He was a bachelor, Raedrick reminded himself. Some men

don't bother with prettying a place up; it took a woman's touch to really make a house into a home. Julian was example enough of that. His rooms were functional and neat, well-maintained. But no one would accuse him of making the place pretty.

All the same, Lester seemed to have taken that to a whole other level. Raedrick wouldn't have thought anyone lived in this room at all, except for the clothes remaining in the cabinet and the fishing man's cloak on the rack.

The place didn't even smell lived-in. It was as though the landlady had cleaned the room up, left a few herbs to hang, and then no one had touched it for a week.

That wasn't what had Raedrick cross though. Crossing his arms over his chest, he tried not to glower at the two men.

"What do you mean, Pat is gone?"

Gilroy and Hiram traded glances, then Gilroy shrugged. "He's nowhere in town. We had every off-duty hand searching. Covered the whole town twice. Every shed, every house, every warehouse. He's not here."

Raedrick looked away from them toward the open window. The stars overhead in the cloudless evening shown brightly, but with the moon not yet risen he could make out few details beyond the glow of lamps in other windows and the mountain range beyond.

It hadn't been that long since the murder; only a few hours. Part of him seethed that the fishing men couldn't have possibly searched everywhere in that time. But the fishing guild had almost a hundred men searching, and Lydelton wasn't really all that large a town.

He drew in a breath. "Ok. When was the last time anyone saw him?"

"At the end of offload this morning," Hiram said. "He told the others on his boat crew he was turning in early so he could be at the speech tonight." He chuckled softly. "Something about intending to pull the rug out from Melton's feet."

Well, someone certainly had done that.

"He lives over by Holb's tavern, right?"

Both men nodded. "We checked there first. Bed's made up neat. Everything's put away. It's like he hadn't been there in a while." Gilroy looked troubled by that; sounded it too.

"That is unusual?"

Hiram chuckled again. "Pat's not exactly the most tidiest of fellows, Constable. Wouldn't remember to coil a rope if one of us didn't remind him to."

Raedrick blinked. That seemed quite an oversight, and the sign of a mindset that he wouldn't have expected from a man as highly regarded on the boats as Pat was.

Hiram must have seen the doubt on his face, because he gave a little shrug as though to take some of the weight from his words.

Raedrick decided to let it lie. "So he left the docks and went home, and no one's seen him since. What about the landlord?"

Shaking heads gave him the answer he expected.

"Well there's not much here to go on either." He gestured toward the cabinet. "Did Lester have any place else he spent time? Doesn't look like he was here much at all."

"Well," Gilroy said, speaking slowly as though trying to spell out his words. "He had a girl."

"<u>Had</u>," Hiram said, putting emphasis on the word.

Raedrick raised an eyebrow.

Gilroy nodded. "Clarice. She's been working with Helena at her school."

Memories of the ghastly murders from a year earlier, and of the hideous beast from another plane of existence that caused them, came flooding back into Raedrick's mind, and he had to suppress a shudder. He worked hard not to think on those events; even now a year later he sometimes replayed them in his dreams.

No rest on those nights.

He knew Helena had continued her and her late sister's craft teaching some of Lydelton's children. Somehow he'd missed that she had taken on help with it, though.

Raedrick pondered for a moment, and a face came to mind. A pretty girl a bit past maturity, long curly blonde hair and a sunny smile. He voiced the description and Gilroy nodded.

"That's her. Lester's been talking about them going to get married in the Fall."

Hiram snorted softly. "Fat chance of that. She was with him, but not <u>with</u> him, if you take my meaning."

"Yeah, well he figured it out and had been moping most of the last week over it." Gilroy looked around the room. "Don't know that he would have kept any things at her place though, even before."

Raedrick frowned. "Did she decide on someone else? Is that what he was sore with Pat over?"

The two men looked at each other and Hiram shrugged. "Don't rightly know. Never seen her and Pat together except in groups."

Well if she had decided she preferred Pat to Lester, that would certainly explain a few things. Women or money tended to be the two things that men Lester's age got into scrapes over the most. If he suspected that was how it was--that Pat had stolen his girl--he would be angry. And he wouldn't need proof of it, either. Some men just came to conclusions, from jealousy or a sense of inferiority, and no need for anything firm to cause it.

That resentment could then flourish and grow until...

But it was Lester who had been killed, not Pat. And now Pat had vanished too.

"Sure makes me think Pat was the one done him in," Gilroy said, giving voice to Raedrick's thoughts. "Lester came at him, they scuffled, and..." He drew his right index finger across his throat in a cutting gesture.

Hiram nodded. "He knew you'd nab him for it, so he skipped town soon as the deed was done."

Raedrick felt his frown growing deeper. "And just leave his girl behind? If she is his girl?" He shook his head. "That doesn't make much sense. If Lester attacked him, we wouldn't string him up over defending himself." He inhaled. "Anyone seen Clarice this evening?"

"I think she's with Helena. She's right upset, to hear tell."

And who could blame her.

"Well. I'll go find her and see what she has to say." Raedrick looked back out the window. The last vestiges of daylight were gone now; only the darkness of night remained. "You two go check all the stables in town. See if there are any horses missing."

Hiram and Gilroy glanced at each other, then nodded, understanding.

Could be Pat added horse thieving to murder.

10

REVELATIONS

The flat that Helena used to share with her late sister, Beverlee, was on the upper floor of a two-story house on the north side of town. A narrow staircase led up from the muddy street to the flat's entrance along the left-hand side of the building. Two of the boards creaked as Raedrick made his way up, one loudly enough that he thought for a moment it was about to give way, and he braced himself, gripping the stairs' handrail firmly for a second.

It wasn't a long fall to the road below, but still...

But the plank held, and Raedrick made a mental note to query Helena as to whether the landlord had been neglecting maintenance. That was something that should have been taken care of a while back, from the sound of things.

Helena opened the door promptly at Raedrick's knock.

She had aged quite a bit in the last year. Her hair had gone fully to grey and there were deeper lines in her face than Raedrick would have thought possible to develop in such a short time.

But it had been a hard year for her. Her sister--her only

companion and best friend--was gone, and she had been working essentially alone to keep up their life's work tending to the town's children. The loneliness and the increased workload, to say nothing of the crushing grief, must have been a heavy burden; heavier than Raedrick could probably understand.

Though he thought he had a better idea of it now, with a new wife and a soon-to-be child, than he did even six months ago.

Helena put on a brave-looking half-smile when the lamp-light from her flat's interior illuminated him in her doorway, and she made a little half-curtsy.

"Evening, Constable," she said. Her dress, blue with white trim, bunched tightly at the waist but flowing loosely about her ankles, made a little rustle as she moved, in time with her words. "I suppose you're looking for Clarice."

There was no surprise in her voice, just certainty of knowledge. And why should there be? Clarice's relationship, or whatever it was, with Lester was hardly a secret.

He nodded. "Is she here?"

Helena stepped aside and gestured with her left hand for him to enter. "She didn't feel up to facing her family, with all that's happened. So I told her she could stay with me for a while."

Raedrick stepped inside. It hadn't changed much since he had last been here. A small kitchen area off to the left, and a table in the center of the room. Chairs and a bookcase on the far wall to the right. High, sloping ceiling that matched the peak of the building's roof. The scent of freshly-brewed herbal tea in the air.

Raedrick took the environs in at a glance, but focused quickly on the girl seated at the eating table, cradling a teacup in clasped hands in front of her.

She was as he recalled: blond and pretty, with a slightly

narrow face and sharp green eyes, which were shadowed by dark emotion as they rose to meet his. Her dress was dark green, and her hair hung loosely to just below her shoulders. Loose, but seemingly freshly combed.

Clarice didn't rise, but nodded at him quickly. "Constable," she said, and sniffed back a break in her voice. "Thought you'd come."

Raedrick walked to the other side of the table, and the simply-carved pine chair that sat there, and she nodded. He sat down and looked at her for a moment before speaking. She was clearly upset, and no wonder.

"I'm sorry about Lester," he said.

Clarice nodded. "Me too. He was a kind person." She frowned, and gave a little shake of her head. "Didn't deserve that."

"I understand you two were close."

She shrugged. "Not as close as he wanted. He..." She trailed off and looked away, toward the door and Helena, still standing there.

"That's part of what I wanted to talk to you about. Word around the fishing guild was you two were going to get engaged, and then you broke it off."

Her short laugh was closer to a half-snort, half-sob, and she shook her head vigorously. "He would say that. I liked him; he was a nice fellow. But never more than that. He assumed my feelings would change, pressed for it. But..." She looked back at Raedrick and made a sad little smile. "You can't control that, can you?"

No, Raedrick supposed not. Still... "Strange that he would tell the other fishing men that, though."

"You had to know him. He was...unsure about how he stood with the other men. Didn't want them to think less of him."

"But you knew he was saying those things?"

A little shrug of her shoulders sent her hair to bouncing slightly. "Seemed harmless enough." She raised the cup to her lips and sipped at her tea. "I didn't encourage it, if that's what you mean."

"Ok. But you broke it off with him completely. Why?"

"Same reason she's here, Constable," Helena said from over his shoulder.

Raedrick blinked and looked back at her. "You said she's staying here temporarily because of the murder."

"I moved in here a week ago."

Raedrick looked back at Clarice and raised an eyebrow. She leaned back a bit, and her left hand went down to her belly. She raised both her eyebrows at him, and he understood.

"Your family didn't take well to that."

She shook her head, her eyes darkening a bit more than they already had been. Raedrick couldn't blame her for that. It must have been quite a blow to take for such a young woman, to be suddenly in trouble and receive no support from her family.

"Who's the father? Pat?"

Clarice did laugh then. Short, bitter-sounding. She shook her head vigorously. "I know Pat to say hello to him, and we've been in gatherings together. But he..." She shook her head again. "I'm not interested."

"Lester seemed to think you and Pat had something going on."

"Lester thought a lot of things that weren't so." There was a bitter tint to her voice as she said that, and Raedrick wondered if she hadn't been as nonchalant about his unwanted advances as she had let on a minute ago.

No wonder if that were the case. It must have grown tiring, keeping Lester at arm's length if he really wouldn't let up. Especially when he'd been talking them up with the other fishing men.

"So who is it?"

Clarice looked at Helena and the two women shared a moment of silence that weighed more than the boulders the Army used to fling from catapults during sieges.

Finally, Clarice made the slightest of nods, and looked back at Raedrick. "Tim Federson."

Raedrick rocked back in his chair, surprise sending his thoughts reeling for a second. "Tim?"

She nodded.

He took a moment to process that. Tim was rather notorious for his charm with the young ladies. But Raedrick had suspected some of that had been a thing Tim himself had fostered to increase his own notoriety. He was a showman.

Still there was no denying he was a bit of the man about town.

"How long have you two been together?"

Clarice looked down at her tea cup. "Not sure as I'd say we've been together, Constable. More like entertaining each other every now and then." Her cheeks turned rosy, the shame of it plain on her face.

Raedrick shifted in his chair a little, suddenly not entirely comfortable. This was one of those awkward subjects... He cleared his throat. "Alright. But now?"

She shrugged slightly. "We were going to wait. Until after the election." Her eyes rose back to meet his, and there was a sudden hardness there. "You know how people are. If they found out..." She shook her head. "I didn't want to be the reason he didn't win."

It seemed less than certain Tim was going to win no matter what. Best not to mention that right this moment though.

Clarice continued. "But now with Pat and Lester... Now it's complicated."

That was putting it mildly. Raedrick sighed and ran his left hand through his hair. He looked back at Helena. "Well I suppose that answers that. Do either of you know where Pat may have gotten to? We can't find him anywhere in town."

Helena opened her mouth to reply but Clarice beat her to it.

"Constable, I'm sure it wasn't him that did in Lester." Her words were sharp, almost desperate-sounding, and Raedrick looked back in her eyes and saw true fear there.

"Maybe. But I still need to find him, to be certain."

Clarice's eyes left Raedrick and flicked toward Helena. From the corner of his eye, he saw the older woman give the smallest of nods.

Clarice swallowed visibly. "Like I said, I didn't know Pat all that well. But he had been hanging around with some folks over at Holb's. Farming men, not his usual fishing mates. I was over there with Tim a week or so ago and heard them talking about a lodge down by the Hook."

"The Hook?" Brice Melton's territory. "You think he went to the Melton Ranch?"

She shook her head. "No, on the lake side of the mountain. Sounded like the kind of thing Povol had built with his hunting lads."

So a retreat, of sorts. A clubhouse for fellows to get away, do some hunting, or whatever this group preferred, without the hustle and bustle of town for a few days.

Not an unappealing notion, now that Raedrick thought on it.

"Do you know where this lodge is?"

She shook her head. "Only heard about it that once."

"Who were these farming men?"

"Mostly fellows I didn't know. But I saw Jeb Tomason come by and talk with them right as Tim and I left."

Jeb Tomason. The rabble rouser from earlier that morning, with the grudge against Brice Melton. He didn't have the kind of money to own a lodge, and would he want to go anywhere near Brice's ranch?

Now that Raedrick thought on it he could think of any number of reasons why the answer to that would be yes, most of them not-so-good. But that wasn't the issue right now; Lester was, and Pat.

"Thanks Clarice," he said. "Looks like Jeb and I get to have another chat." He went to rise from his chair, but she stabbed a hand out and clamped onto his forearm with soft fingers that gripped like a little vice.

"You aren't going to tell anyone about...?" Her eyes lowered toward her belly, and she flushed again.

Raedrick shook his head.

Her shoulders slumped a little, in relief he thought, and she nodded, releasing his arm.

He stood, scraping the chair softly against the flat's floorboards as he moved. "Thank you, ladies," he said, and Helena nodded in reply.

He followed her to the door, his mind shifting to consider his next move. Jeb had a room over at Bigsbe's. Easy to find him. Go now or - ?

A sudden yawn made him stop as he stepped out onto the stairs outside Helena's flat, and he looked up at the twinkling stars above. He blinked, then looked back at Helena where she was silhouetted in the doorway.

He hadn't realized how late it really was, and he felt a flush of shame sweep over him. "I'm sorry about the hour. But thank you."

Helena smiled faintly at him. "Get some rest, Constable. You look about out on your feet."

And right then he realized he felt it, too. He'd been charging all evening, but in that moment it was like the drive to go on just flowed right out, and weariness swept over him. He nodded.

"I think I may do that," he said. "Good night."

She made a little nod his way, and he turned to descend the stairs.

He really needed to talk to Jeb.

In the morning.

11

JEB

*J*eb's eyes were bloodshot, like he had been up late and drinking hard. Which he probably had been. He looked up at Raedrick from where he sat on the side of the little cot he had set up in his room in Bigsbe's Boarding House, its blankets threadbare wool that may once have been died blue but now were at best grey.

He was still wearing his nightclothes, a long off-white cotton shirt that stretched to his knees and was unlaced halfway down his chest, and his hair was tussled and unruly. The look he alternated between Raedrick, Gilroy, and Hiram was disgruntled and bitter, as though he clearly wished he could summon the will to make it threatening but instead all he could manage was a semi-frown that merely turned petulant.

Raedrick had roused himself early--earlier than he wanted to, and far earlier than his body screamed at him to do--but had already found the two fishing men up and eager to be about their duties assisting him.

Part of him had wanted to scream at them for their high energy this early on in the day, but he had shoved that aside in favor of admiration, and an acknowledgement of the discipline that came from their enforced early days out on the boats to make the morning catch before the sun rose too high in the sky and the fish went deep for the day.

They had made the short walk from the Constabulary to Bigsbe's after only a brief conference, and found Jeb still soundly asleep when they pounded on his door.

Perfect. Much less likely he would try to snow them if he wasn't entirely in his proper frame of mind yet.

And so they had barged in and now stood in a half-circle around his bed as he tried and failed to look anything but tired, hung over, and impotently resentful.

"Told you, Constable, I didn't have nothing to do with Lester," Jeb said. Again.

"Wasn't asking about that, Jeb," Raedrick said. Again. "I was asking about the lodge you and Pat have down by the Hook."

Jeb rolled his eyes. "I don't have a lodge. I - "

"Then you know who does, and you probably know where it is."

Jeb worked his jaw for a few seconds, then gave a reluctant grunt and a half-nod of acknowledgement at Raedrick's state-ment. "Ain't no big secret, Constable. A dozen or so folks got together and made it, just like Povol and them did. That's not illegal." He put a bit of resentful pushback into that last.

Raedrick nodded. "Didn't say it was. Where is it?"

"Like you said, down by the Hook. You know where the moun-tain comes down almost to the road along the lake? About two miles east of there, and up the mountain a ways, in the woods."

It had been a while since Raedrick had been down that way. In fact, it had been since he and Julian first arrived, traveling east from Calas. But he recalled there wasn't as much forestation on that side of the lake as the north side, where Lydelton lay. Stray copses and some more dense woods up along the flanks of the mountains. But it was mostly rolling grassland from the East-flow down to the Hook.

Shouldn't make the lodge all that difficult to find.

"Anything else?"

Jeb shrugged. "They made a little path from the road. Marked it with stones, like the road has. Door's normally locked; only the fellows as own it have keys."

Raedrick looked back at Hiram and Gilroy and saw they were thinking the same thing he was. Time to take a little trip.

"Alright. Thanks, Jeb. You may have just helped us find a murderer."

Jeb blinked, then his face brightened slightly. "Happy to do my duty, Constable."

Hiram gave a little half-snort, then they trooped out of Jeb's room and the Boarding House.

On the street outside, Raedrick paused and looked up at the sun. It was just rising above the steeply-slanting rooftops to the west of Bigsbe's, far from its zenith in a sky that was filled with puffy clouds that spoke of the possibility of rain later, but not a large one.

He took a moment to work the hour in his head--and inwardly heard Julian's voice poking fun at him for how much longer it took him than Julian thought it should--and frowned.

"Five or six hours down there at least," he said, and turned down the cross street leading from Bigsbe's to Main Street, and then the Oarlock where he kept his horse. "An hour or two to find the lodge and rouse Pat... It'll be almost midnight by the time we get back. No time to waste."

From behind him and to his left, Gilroy said, "Won't take near that long, Constable."

Raedrick looked back and crooked an eyebrow at him, and Gilroy chuckled. He stopped and pointed down the cross street toward where it continued past Main and down toward the lake, and the docks.

The ground sloped down toward the lake the whole way and from this angle fishing boats were clearly visible, returning for the morning offload. The dark blue water of the lake was lapping with two or three foot waves, sparkling with reflected sunlight, and past, distant but clearly visible, the encroaching mountains that made up the Hook stood out, almost exactly on the opposite side of the lake from Lydelton.

"Good wind this morning," Gilroy continued, "out of the east. Should be able to cross in two, maybe three hours."

Raedrick blinked. It wasn't that he had anything against boats. He'd sailed in plenty over the years. But he didn't spend much time out on the water, and when it came to travel he naturally defaulted to thinking in terms of horses or carts. He hadn't even considered the idea, but Gilroy was right. A direct crossing would save a lot of time.

"We'd have to walk when we get there."

"What, afraid your feet will get sore?" Hiram said, a note of teasing in his voice.

Raedrick snorted, but couldn't help grinning back at him in acknowledgement of the joke. "It'll take longer is all," he said. Looking back at the lake, another thought occurred to him. "Looks like the boats are all taken though."

"Plenty of others we can use," Gilroy said. "Horace has his own. Or," he grinned widely, a twinkle in his eye, "maybe you can ask the Mayor for his. Right nice little sailer she is."

Another thing Raedrick hadn't considered. He had known plenty of people in town--the more well to do mostly but a few of the common folk as well--had little pleasure launches. And he had seen Brimly out on his boat a time or two. Gilroy was right; it was nice, and almost as large as the working boats the Covington Brothers' company used.

But no, he shook his head. "Let's ask Horace for his."

Gilroy looked disappointed, but he nodded agreement. Turning on his heel, he led the way down toward the lake, and the docks. "He's normally the first one in to coordinate offload," he said. "Shouldn't take but a few minutes and we should be underway. Can dock down at Melton's place."

More surprises. "Melton has a dock?"

Hiram nodded. "He made it about a year ago. Saves him time getting his produce and meats up here to market." He grinned slyly. "Covington Brothers are getting nervous about it. Think he might start his own fishing fleet down there one day."

Which wouldn't necessarily be a bad thing, Raedrick considered. The Covington Brothers had a lock on the fishing in Lake Glimmermere. Competition could only be good for the people who worked the trade, and for commerce at large in Glimmer Vale.

Then again, there was already tension between Melton and the other farmers in the Vale; Jeb was proof enough of that. Would expanding into the fishing arena drive a wedge deeper between Melton's camp and the rest of the people?

Maybe that was why he was running for Mayor. To head that off before it grew too extreme and would interfere with his more grandiose plans.

Which made Raedrick curious what he would say later on this evening; he hadn't had a chance to fully lay his plan out yesterday before Lester's murder interrupted things.

"Ok let's get to it," Raedrick said.

The sooner they got underway, the more likely to get back before speech time.

12

CROSSING OVER

*H*orace's boat was, naturally, well kept. But also quite a bit more comfortable than Raedrick would have expected. A little bit over twenty feet in length, it boasted a single mast that supported a mainsail on a boom behind the mast and a triangular forward sail...jib...whatever it was the fishing men called it. It had a covered area up forward large enough for a small table desk and a cot, and benches for seating up topside. The steering was done with a tiller at the rear.

The boat was painted blue with white trim above the water-line, the tiller capped with a brass handle that gleamed in the sunlight from many hours of Horace's polishing. The rigging was taught, the ropes well kept...all in all, a first class vessel, as far as Raedrick could tell.

As he stood alongside the mast, one hand on it to brace himself against the boat's heeling as it drove through the lake's waves, and watched the peaks of the Hook draw implacably nearer, Raedrick couldn't help but be impressed.

Horace had been only too glad to lend them the boat...as soon as he realized it was Hiram and Gilroy who would be driving it, not Raedrick.

"No offense Constable, but you are never taking Heather out by yourself," the old fishing man had said, the earnest look in his eye showing he meant every word--and was not joking around one bit.

Raedrick had thought to protest for a moment. But only for a moment. He knew his limitations.

And watching the two fishing men smoothly and efficiently raise the sails, untie the boat from the dock, and get her underway, he knew he could never have accomplished the same feat. At least not without at least half a dozen mishaps and while taking four times as long.

Now, as they were nearing the end of their crossing, it was clear this had been the right choice. The wind had kept up nicely all morning; in fact it had grown a bit stronger, increasing their speed...and the angle of the boat's heeling. Raedrick couldn't help but be a bit nervous at first, until the fishing men helped set him straight.

"We ain't even on a close haul, and he's turning green."

"Relax, Constable. My four year old's seen worse weather than this."

A few minutes of that, and Raedrick resolved to buck up; or at least make it look like he was.

It had apparently worked, and now their destination was clearly in sight.

The northernmost mountain of the Hook--Raedrick didn't know if it had a name or not--was rearing up ahead of them and to the right. Trees graced its flanks a few dozen yards up, but down where it merged into the lake it was mostly clear grassland, just as Raedrick remembered from his earlier travels.

There, meandering from right to left across the lowest portion of the mountain's flank, was the road running up toward Lydelton and then the pass to Mangin City, and the other way toward the Silver Falls, Garrett's Gorge, and the town of Calas in the plains beyond the Saddleback Mountains. The packed earth of the road stood out easily against the waving green of the grasslands, and Raedrick could see a cart clopping along it coming from the direction of Lydelton.

A farmer returning back from market, or one of Melton's men perhaps?

Impossible to tell, and anyway as Raedrick's eyes followed the cart he zeroed in on the target of this day's voyage.

Melton's dock was actually a trio of finger piers attached to shore by a common walkway. Sturdy-looking, constructed from thick timbers, it looked well-made and built to endure. There were two boats tied up along the finger piers as they approached, their low-hulled, bulky design clearly made more for hauling cargo than for speed, or for fishing.

So it looked like the Covington Brothers had nothing to worry about. For now, at least.

"Beg pardon, Constable," Hiram said from behind him, and Raedrick flinched slightly as his contemplation of the scene was broken. He glanced back at Hiram, and he grinned and pointed upwards toward the top of the mast. "Time to lower the jib. Don't want to run into the pier, right?"

Raedrick chuckled and stepped away from the mast, and back down into the steering cockpit at the rear of the boat with Gilroy.

"Always touchy coming in to the dock," Gilroy said. He stood to the right of the tiller and was focused straight ahead, his eyes squinting slightly as he watched the approaching construction. "Wait too long getting the sails down and you run into it. Damage your boat and look like an idiot. Take them down too early and you run out of speed before you get there. You're stuck, and look like an idiot." He glanced aside at Raedrick and flashed him a jolly smile. "Don't want to look like an idiot, do we?"

Oh so that was the important part, was it?

Up forward, Hiram had the front sail--the jib?--down on deck and was bunching it up in a manner that looked at first glance that it must make the thing into an unruly heap, but after a few seconds Raedrick saw that he was in fact adroitly bundling it into a compact, neat bundle. It only took him a short time to get the bundle tied down, then he stepped back to the mast and looked at Gilroy.

On the dock ahead, a pair of men had emerged from a little shack at the head of the finger piers. They were dressed in loose-fitting brown pants and off-white tunics with their cuffs rolled up. The men moved with quick strides down the right-most of the finger piers; the one Gilroy was heading toward, which was free of boats.

"Nice of Melton to put a lot of space between the piers," Gilroy said, making a small adjustment on the tiller. "Some of the docks up in Lydelton you almost have to hit the boat on the next pier to get in."

"I'm sure he was thinking just about you when he did it," Hiram said from the mast, and Gilroy chuckled.

"Ahoy!" came a shout from the leading man on the pier. He had a baritone voice that sounded young, though from the extensive beard that luxuriated on his chest Raedrick gave him at least thirty to thirty-five years.

"Hello the dock," Gilroy shouted back. He adjusted the tiller again, and the boat bore slightly to the right, so that it was now pointed almost right at the place where the finger pier met the walkway at the end. Then he nodded quickly at Hiram.

Hiram returned the nod and loosed the rope holding the mainsail, and the canvas dropped.

Almost at once the boat began to slow noticeably. Very noticeably.

Gilroy's second horror-scenario, the lesser of the two in

Raedrick's opinion, sprang to mind, and Raedrick began to wonder if they were going to make it all the way.

"What brings you to the Melton wharf?" asked the bearded man from the dock.

Gilroy rolled his eyes slightly. "They always pry," he said to Raedrick in a low tone of voice that wouldn't carry. Then he spoke up. "Official business of the Constable." He gestured with his free hand toward Raedrick, who lifted his right hand in greeting.

The two men on the dock traded looks, then the one who hadn't spoken yet split off from beard man and moved toward the front end of the approaching boat. Beard man walked slowly toward the rear.

"Docking fee still applies," said bearded man. "Even for the Constable."

"Docking fee?" Raedrick asked, surprised. There was no fee to dock at the Lydelton town docks. Money for maintenance of the docks came from duties the town imposed on caravans and on the sale of the Covington Brothers' fish.

Hiram was finishing lashing the main sail into place atop the mast's boom. He glanced up at Raedrick as he pulled one of the sail ties tight and sneered. "Melton always finds a way to milk some money out of you," he said. Then he turned and headed to the front of the boat, where a rope lay coiled around a little post mounted there.

He lifted the rope so the man on the dock could see, and he responded by raising his hand.

Hiram tossed the coiled end of the rope over, holding on to the loose end, and it sailed across the now much reduced distance between boat and dock.

The man on the dock caught it, and began lashing it to a post on the dock.

And the rear of the boat, Gilroy tossed beard man another

line, and in just a few moments the boat was secured at both ends, its middle gently bumping up against the canvas-padded posts of the dock in time with the lake's wave motion.

The two men on the dock--they were close enough now for Raedrick to see that the silent one was more boy than man--if he was sixteen Raedrick was fifty--dragged a plank of wood, flat on one said with raised ridges of wood nailed into the other side every few inches--to give grip while walked on it Raedrick supposed--over to the end of the dock, then plopped one end of the plank down on the boat's mid section.

Then they gestured for Raedrick and company to come ashore.

As Raedrick stepped off the plank onto the dock, beard man stepped up and extended his hand. "Good to meet you, Constable. I'm Avery Damons." Raedrick clasped hands with Avery and found his grip firm, his palms heavily callused.

Avery nodded at the young man, who had come up to join them. This close, there was an obvious resemblance between the two. Round faces, broad shoulders--though the younger man could still do with a lot of filling out--dark brown eyes and the hair to match.

"My son, Jac," Avery said, confirming Raedrick's suspicion.

Raedrick clasped hands with Jac, then turned his attention back to Avery. "How much is the docking fee?"

"Five pennies a day," Avery said, sounding almost apologetic.

"That doesn't seem too terribly bad," Raedrick said, looking back at Hiram and Gilroy, who had joined them on the dock.

"It ain't," Hiram said. "Except Melton's boats don't have to pay, do they?"

Avery shrugged. "Can't expect the man to charge himself, can you?"

Which was fair enough, Raedrick supposed. He reached into his belt pouch, where he kept his money, and counted out the fee. He'd invoice the Mayor's office for reimbursement later on.

"We should only be a few hours," he said as he handed the money over.

Avery counted it, then nodded. "Well this'll keep you til noon tomorrow, if you need."

That was good to know. "I don't come down here to the Hook that often," Raedrick began, and Avery nodded agreement.

There was something in the dockmaster's eyes when he nodded that gave Raedrick pause.

"There a problem?"

Avery shrugged again. "Not so you'd say it, Constable. But lot of people down here feel like the law's abandoned them."

An echo of Melton's words from the other day. Raedrick felt himself flushing slightly.

"Yes well, I've been neglectful in that respect. I plan to change that; this visit is the start."

Avery nodded, a mixture of doubt and hopefulness showing through in his face for a moment.

No point in pressing the matter, though. "Anyway, we are looking for a fugitive. Think he may be hiding out in a lodge up on the lake side of the mountain's flank." He pointed toward the peak rearing up, much nearer now and more imposing, off to the right. "Owned by a group of farming types, as I understand it."

Avery's brow furrowed, and he followed Raedrick's gesture toward the mountain. He frowned and shook his head, looking back at Raedrick with a questioning expression. "Don't know as I'm aware of a lodge up there, Constable. Only homesteads nearer than Master Melton's ranch are the Hemfields and the McAlisters, but they're off to the east a ways, not on the mountain."

Raedrick frowned. The lodge couldn't be that secret. If it was here, the owners would have had to get supplies from time to time. Melton's ranch, or one of the other farmsteads, would be the obvious place to go for them. And so surely the locals would have word at least of the lodge's existence?

But then again, Avery's concern was the dock, not the mountainside. He just may simply have never had need to come across word of it. Surely Jeb's friends would not have sailed down here; they would have taken the road to get to it.

So maybe not an issue that Avery wouldn't know about it.

Still, odd. And as he glanced back at Gilroy and Hiram he could tell they thought the same.

Drawing a quick breath, he turned his attention back on Avery. "Well we'll figure it out. Thanks for your help, Avery."

"What I'm here for, Constable." Avery gestured toward a spot on the shore and about a hundred yards to the west of the docks, where a small cabin made from cleanly-hewn logs, with a steep thatch roof and a single stone fireplace, stood a couple dozen yards back from the lakeshore. "Most folks don't leave dock after sunset, but if you have a need, knock and we'll come assist."

"I'll do that, thanks."

They clasped hands again, then Raedrick turned toward the walkway to the shore, and then to the road.

13

HIKING

"*D*oes it seem strange to you that Avery had never heard of this lodge?" Raedrick asked.

They had reached the road and turned to the right, in the direction of the mountain. It was slower going than he would have liked; the road was still soft from the previous rain, and traffic was more sparse down here than up near Lydelton so it wasn't as well-packed either.

But the sun was high, nearing its zenith, and the easterly wind kept the normal midday heat to a pleasant warmth. The grass on either side of the road bent gently below the gusts, wildflowers adding extra bits of color to the otherwise pristine green of the immediate area. An earthy odor--dirt and growth with a hint of sweetness--filled the air, and Raedrick couldn't help feeling energized by it.

To his right, Hiram shrugged. "I get the feeling Jeb's friends didn't spread word of it too far. Can't say I blame them."

True enough. Still...

Raedrick peered ahead at the mountain, to where it swept down into the lake, maybe three or four miles ahead. "I suppose we'll find out soon enough. Jeb said it was a couple miles east of that point, so we should find their path any minute now. Keep an eye out."

The road ran more or less straight, but began a slow rise as it approached the mountain's flank. After a few minutes of traveling, Raedrick glanced back and beheld a more expansive vista of the land to the east and south.

The road going east was easy to make out, as was a second heading south that broke off about a mile and a half from where they were. The road to Melton's ranch, presumably. That cart that he had seen approaching as they docked had turned onto the southern road. Further east, a few plumes of smoke rose into the sky; the chimneys from several of the scattered farming homesteads in the southern half of the Vale.

Was it his imagination, or were there more now than when he first came through here with Julian, a year and a half ago?

Small surprise if that was the case. Isenholf's band of brigands was raiding the area then; they no longer were. But he had not given any thought to what had happened to the population in the rest of the Vale outside Lydelton in the last year. The town's population had grown slightly, he knew. Or at least, he suspected.

But the rest of the Vale?

Maybe it was time to do true census of the Vale. It had been a long time since the last one; since well before Raedrick and Julian had come.

Especially if Melton won and began enacting his plans. The Kingdom's tax collectors had been lax the last many years in collection of the Vale's duties. Mayor Brimly had made that plain earlier this year, and that he had been collecting the taxes anyway in expectation that someday the Kingdom would want its money--in full.

But if the population had truly grown substantially, if Melton succeeded in getting the Vale back onto the Kingdom's map it could be even Brimly's preparations might not be enough.

Something to think on. And talk with the Mayor about.

"Have a look here, Constable," said Gilroy, from up ahead.

Raedrick realized he had fallen behind the two fishing men in his contemplation of the scene. He turned back and hurried over to where they now stood next to a small pile of stones on the south side of the road.

The pile resembled the distance markers that were placed along the road itself at regular intervals. But those markers were made of neatly-placed rocks that had been shaped to fit well together and that stood about four feet in height.

This pile was more slipshod, and only stood about a foot and a half high. Just barely tall enough to rise above the grass on the side of the road.

The grass there looked as though it had been disturbed a few times in the past. It wasn't enough to call it a second road, or even really a path. More like some of the grass had been beaten down extending in a roughly uniform direction to the south and west away from the main road.

"That matches what Jeb said," Gilroy said as Raedrick stepped up next to him and Hiram.

"Sort of," Hiram added wryly.

Raedrick nodded agreement. "Let's see."

They left the road and began pushing through the grass. It was clear others had come through this way recently; several others, as the grass was beaten down in a line roughly four feet wide. But there hadn't been enough traffic to truly make a path of it, and although beaten the grass had not been defeated, and it hampered their progress, making what had been an easy walk into an exertion.

The "path" also began to rise more steeply than the road had. The road followed the shore of Lake Glimmermere across the lower flank of the mountain as it pushed up toward the lake. This route seemed to be going almost directly up the mountain, and It didn't help that the wind had been growing more weak as they ascended. Very quickly Raedrick found he was sweating from the effort of the climb, and his breath was coming in quick heaves.

Beside him, Gilroy's greater bulk was giving him a harder time of it; he was huffing and puffing loudly while sweat poured down his forehead and wetted his shirt obviously.

Raedrick slowed to let the fishing man have an easier go, and he flashed a grateful grin. "Not used to this kind of thing," he said. "Plenty of work to do on the boats, but not a lot of climbing."

"Speak for yourself," said the more spry Hiram behind them, though when Raedrick looked back at him he was flushed and also gulping in air, if sweating a bit less than Gilroy was. He looked cheerful enough, though.

Raedrick could relate. Though his duties had him moving around on his feet much of the day, he rarely got out into the hills and mountains of the Vale. He made a mental note to change that. If even this relatively short climb was turning out to be such an effort...

"On the bright side," Raedrick said as he lifted a suddenly heavy foot, "we're almost to the tree line."

And a good thing, too.

The change once they passed beneath the bows of the first pines was like night and day; almost literally. The shade was an immediate relief from the sun's warmth, but Raedrick found himself blinking to help his eyes adjust to the suddenly dimmer light.

They paused for a few minutes to catch their breath and to just enjoy the blessed coolness.

"Shoulda brought some water skins," Hiram said after a

moment, a rueful expression on his face, and Raedrick nodded in glum agreement.

There had been a water cask on the Heather, but he hadn't considered how strenuous the journey to the lodge might be so he hadn't thought to bring any along. Stupid.

"Well it shouldn't be too much farther," Raedrick said, and nodded uphill a short ways and to the left, where another pile of stones stood.

Here beneath the trees' canopy there was no grass to trample, just some underbrush and fallen pine needles atop the dirt. It made for a fine, relaxing odor on the air, but it also made for fewer signs to show a path, especially one as infrequently used as this one obviously was. So they would have to be more attentive to those stone piles, otherwise they might wander astray and miss their goal entirely.

The two fishing men grunted out acknowledging nods, and though it was plain they would much rather spend some more time at rest, they drew themselves erect and proceeded to follow Raedrick toward the path marker.

The path continued more or less straight for another quarter hour or so, then veered to the right, almost doubling back on itself in order to run parallel with the ridge's contour instead of challenging the mountain straight on like it had been.

And thank the gods for that.

After a time, the trees began to thin, the underbrush grew more dense, and Raedrick could spy a clearing up ahead. Bright sunlight streaming down shown like a beacon in the comforting shade, and he felt almost drawn toward it, like it was beckoning to him.

Small wonder that the path markers led straight toward it.

But as they drew nearer to the clearing, Raedrick slowed. There was something...off. Not right.

The pine needle scent remained on the air, just as strong as it had been. A very slight breeze blew in from downhill and to the east, just enough to notice but not enough to really make an impact.

Up head, a series of bushes had grown up around the last few trees, obscuring most of the view, but it was plain to see where the path led, straight through a gap between two of them. In the gap he could just make out the grass and wildflowers of a meadow, and further on the kinds of straight lines that could only come from men's handiwork.

At last, they'd found it.

He went to move forward, but again that sense of wrongness seeped in, and he hesitated.

It was then he realized it. The woods were silent. Before there had been the ubiquitous sounds of life: insects buzzing, birds on the wing, small creatures rustling across the ground-- everywhere and nowhere so that they almost didn't register at all, they were so constant.

Not here.

He frowned and stopped, making a silent gesture with his hands for his companions to do the same.

They looked at him, Gilroy with a quirked eyebrow, Hiram with his head cocked to the side, inquiringly.

Raedrick pointed ahead toward the gap, then pantomimed drawing a bow.

The fishing men nodded immediate understanding. They each had brought bows from the cache at the Constabulary. Hiram had also brought a sword. Now they unlimbered the weapons and strung their bowstrings. Nocked arrows.

They nodded at him, indicating readiness, and he drew his sword.

He had grown much more comfortable with this weapon over the last six months or so. It was of fine Tyrashi make, bequeathed to him by Selam, the most gifted swordsman

Raedrick had ever fought beside. Gracefully curved, its weight and balance were different enough from the saber Raedrick had preferred before coming to the Vale that it had taken a while for him to become adequate with the new blade.

Even now he didn't feel he had reached his prior level of skill, but it almost felt a part of him and that was much improved from a year ago.

The curved blade gleamed in front of him, reflecting a hint of the sunlight from the clearing ahead, and he placed his left hand below his right on the hand-and-a-half hilt of the sword. Then he started forward.

He reached the gap quickly, and paused to look beyond.

The lodge--really a small cabin made from rough-hewn logs; very small--lay on the far side of the clearing, maybe fifty feet away. Its entrance faced them, and it backed up to a cluster of pines so close together they almost could have been a wall unto themselves. The entrance door was in the center of the front wall, and a single window was carved in to the door's right. The roof was steep, as all roofs in the Vale had to be to weather winter's heavy snowfalls, and made from thatch that looked freshly laid.

Raedrick took all that in at a glance, but focused in on two things.

The window was glass, and shattered. And the door was hanging open, dangling halfheartedly from one hinge that looked ready to give out at any second.

Raedrick looked to the side at Gilroy. The fishing man's expression--a mixture of caution, worry, and chagrin--spoke volumes.

Raedrick felt the same.

14
______

MOUNTAIN LODGE

A growl followed by a series of yips greeted Raedrick and the fishing men as they neared the battered front door of the cabin. It came from within, and Raedrick immediately recognized it. Coyote. A couple of them.

Made sense, they would hunt when they could manage it, but they were not above scavenging. And from the odor as they neared the cabin there was easy meat available inside.

Hiram and Gilroy slowed upon hearing the beasts' call, Gilroy swallowing visibly and going a bit pale.

"They are not courageous creatures," Raedrick said, recalling a discussion he had with Povol the woodsman some months back.

"But they'll fight if we corner them," Hiram said, craning his neck to look around the cabin's front wall. "If there's a back door...?"

Raedrick nodded quickly. "Check."

Hiram grimaced but nodded. He eased his bowstring and set the weapon down, then drew his sword. Moving quickly through the meadow grass, he sped to the right and vanished beyond the corner of the cabin.

Meanwhile, Raedrick turned back toward the front door, flexing his fingers on the grip of his sword.

The doorway was a hole of blackness in the sunlight; nothing was visible within, though he could now hear the creatures' movement easily.

Another yip came out, and Gilroy drew halfway back on his arrow.

Raedrick nodded at him. "Be ready." He moved forward, toward the right side of the broken doorway, where the window lay, the bottom of its frame just above chin height.

From the corner of his eye, he saw Gilroy move directly in front of the door, about fifteen feet back, and he raised his bow to sight down the arrow's shaft.

Raedrick reached the window and peeked inside.

From this close, the sunlight entering through the window and the open doorway cast partial illumination on the interior. He could see a bunkbed on the far wall and a table off to the right. A shadowy shape was lying on the ground between them, with three smaller shadows moving around it.

A body perhaps, and three of the scavenging creatures, no doubt interrupted in their meal.

His mouth twisted in disgust and he considered that he could probably drive the coyotes away if he moved fast enough. Maybe. Or maybe they would turn on him. Could he fight three of them off?

One of the scavengers looked to bite into part of the shape on the floor, and he decided it was worth the risk. Whoever that was, he didn't deserve to be disgraced so.

Raedrick drew a deep breath. He opened his mouth to call out for Gilroy to cover him...

And a new source of illumination shed light into the interior of the cabin. From the left wall, near the foot of the bunkbeds. Another door opening from the outside.

And then Hiram's voice pierced the air, a loud shout that came with a stomping of booted feet on wood.

The creatures surrounding the body stiffened, and Raedrick saw their ears point up on their heads.

Hiram shouted again, and something came crashing into the room from the second door, and the coyotes broke.

Yipping loudly, they bolted out the front door, bounding past Raedrick, who flattened himself against the exterior wall as they ran past.

Gilroy let out a yelp of his own, followed by the twang of a released bowstring, then the whistle of an arrow in flight.

One of the creatures let out another yelp--of pain, not panic--and fell sprawling in the grass a short distance to Raedrick's left. The other two kept on going past Gilroy, who turned to watch them go with a look of startled amazement mixed with chagrin mixed with fright, and disappeared in the underbrush on the far side of the meadow.

The wounded animal let out a long whimper, squirming on the grass but unable to move from the arrow that had pierced its side.

Raedrick blinked, his thoughts coalescing together in a jerk as he took in the rapid series of events, then he looked from the downed coyote to Gilroy.

"Nice shot," he said, and walked over to the wounded animal.

"Thanks," Gilroy said, sounding surprised. Almost shocked, actually.

And no wonder. He had apparently shot by reflex as much as anything else, and still managed to hit a creature at a run without much time at all to aim.

Part of Raedrick wanted to upgrade him for shooting so close to where he had been standing; it would have been easy to miss, and then there would be a Constable on the ground, not a coyote. But you can't argue with results.

He stopped a couple feet from the downed coyote. It squirmed in the grass, obviously pained. Its grey-brown coat red from the blood flowing from around the arrow shaft. It wasn't long for this world, but no need for it to suffer.

A sword stroke finished it, then Raedrick turned back to the cabin.

Hiram was standing in the doorway. His sword was back in its scabbard, but he looked grim. "Bit of a mess inside. There was a fight of some kind. Not sure who or how many."

"The body?"

Hiram snorted, and shook his head. "A side of salted meat, looks like."

Raedrick blinked. "Come again?"

Hiram shrugged. "See for yourself."

Raedrick clumped through the open doorway. He paused to let his eyes adjust to the gloom, but immediately he could see that Hiram was correct. What he had thought was a human body from outside was in fact a large hunk of meat, probably venison as this was presumably a hunting cabin. It was white with salt except for where the coyotes had gnawed on it, and a few smaller places where clean cuts had removed some of the meat.

He glanced to the right, to where a plainly-constructed table, surrounded by a quartet of chairs, sat. There was a plate atop the table with a hunk of meat--from this larger piece no doubt--on it. It had pieces obviously cut from it, and a fork was stuck into the top of it.

A tumbled-over chair next to the table added to the tale; whatever happened here, it had occurred right at dinner time.

He looked back at the meat on the floor. It had been hung up by a strand of rope, looked like. But the rope was cut. A smooth cut; not much unravelling to it.

So someone had used a blade on it.

Raedrick frowned, taking the scene in as he considered.

"Last anyone saw Pat was yesterday morning at offload," he said. He looked over at Hiram. "No horses missing from the stables, you said?"

Hiram shook his head. "None that shouldn't have been gone. And before you ask, lots of folks took their animals out yesterday. Every day, in fact, from what the hands said. Nothing stood out as unusual."

"Anyone from down here by the Hook?"

Hiram shrugged and spread his hands helplessly.

Of course he wouldn't have thought to ask that. There was no reason he should have. Raedrick sighed.

"Well assuming he went with someone from down here using their horses; or maybe he stole the person's horse after they took it out of the stable. He would have gotten here about three or four hours before dark."

"Unless he didn't leave until after he killed Lester," Hiram said.

Raedrick looked at him, and the fishing man shrugged. "Don't know as he didn't do it yet, do we?"

"True enough." But if he had killed Lester and then made off down here... "But if that's the case he couldn't have gotten here until well after midnight."

The other two men frowned, but nodded agreement.

That didn't leave much room in the timeline of events. Someone had clearly come while Pat had been eating. And it looked like there had been a scuffle of some sort. But why would the assailants have attacked then, and how would they have known Pat was even here?

Or was it just random chance, a break-in for loot that went awry?

But even an incompetent robber could tell whether the building he intended to break into was occupied. Especially a small place like this. No, they had to know Pat was here. So either they were after him or they thought they could easily overpower him and take what they wanted.

But that would mean leaving a witness. And...

But aside from the meat on the floor and the overturned chair, it didn't look like much had been disturbed here.

"Doesn't look like they searched the place at all," he said out loud.

The fishing men shook their heads. Gilroy was sucking on his lip in thought. From his expression he didn't like the conclusion he was coming to.

Neither did Raedrick.

"So they came here just for Pat. Which means they knew he was here; maybe waited on him."

"Something's right fishy about this whole thing," Gilroy said.

Raedrick nodded. The entire caper was becoming more convoluted by the second.

15

MELTON RANCH

There was no sign of Avery and Jac on the docks when Raedrick, Gilroy, and Hiram returned.

The day's heat had only increased during their trek back, especially after they left the relative coolness of the forest's canopy. And by the time they reached the ramp leading up to the finger piers, Raedrick's shirt was sticking to his body from the sweat that had been pouring off him.

He wanted nothing more than to just hop back aboard Horace's boat and get back underway; the cooling breeze on the water beckoned to him. But there was the mystery of what happened at the lodge, and where the people who had taken Pat had made off to.

So instead of mounting the dock, he instead turned left toward Avery and Jac's little cabin. There was smoke rising from the fireplace; perhaps they were preparing afternoon tea, or getting an early start on their evening meal. It was still several hours til sunset, earlier than most people up Lydelton-way had dinner. But maybe their duties required a different schedule, or they just preferred it early.

Either way.

"What are we doing, Constable?" Hiram asked as they trouped toward the cabin.

"They live along the road. Maybe one of them saw what happened," he said.

In the silence from the two fishing men behind him, he could practically feel their shrugs.

Avery and Jac's cabin was sturdily-built from hewn pine logs. There were no windows at the front, and the door was solid-looking, plainly carved but well-sanded and stained a light brown.

He rapped on the door with a rapid three blows of his fist. It opened a moment later to reveal Avery, with the sleeves of his tunic rolled up to his biceps and his collar unlaced against the day's warmth.

He nodded in greeting. "Constable. Looks like you've had a hard time of it."

Raedrick grinned at the comment; no doubt he looked as drained as he felt. "Sorry to disturb you, Avery," he began, and the dockmaster waved his comment off.

"Always happy to help."

"Yes, well, we found the lodge. Our fugitive wasn't there but it looked like he had been. There were signs of a scuffle. Looks like someone rousted him and took him out of there by force."

Avery's eyebrows rose. "Not one of your people, I take it?"

Raedrick shook his head. "It must have happened sometime last night. Did you see anything?"

Avery pursed his lips, then shook his head. "Can't say I did. But I turn in early these days. The years are starting to get to me." He grinned in self-deprecating humor and chuckled softly at his own quip. Then he turned to look behind himself. "Jac! Constable's got a question for you."

Jac stepped up beside his father, his youthful features curious as he looked Raedrick over.

Raedrick repeated the question, and Jac nodded immediately. "I stayed up a bit later than normal last night with a book. I went to the outhouse a bit before midnight and saw some men riding from the west. Two or three of them, on horses with torches."

"You didn't mention that before," Avery said, looking at his son askance.

Jac shrugged. "Didn't think anything of it. People are always on the road."

Raedrick doubted there was all <u>that</u> much traffic on the road, as sparsely populated as the Vale was and as infrequent as caravans were. Especially at night. But Jac had a point; there was no reason to assume something untoward just from that.

"Where did they go?"

Jac shrugged. "I didn't follow them, but it looked like they took the fork down to the Melton ranch."

Behind him, Gilroy and Hiram shuffled on their feet. No doubt they found that revelation as interesting as Raedrick did. If those horsemen were the ones who had taken Pat, and they worked for Melton...

That screamed suspicious.

"How far is it to the ranch from here?"

Avery spoke up. "Good hour on foot, around the flank of the mountain into the heart of the Hook." He paused, and must have seen the expression on Raedrick's face as he contemplated yet another long hike in the day's heat, because Avery said, "We've got a cart around back you can use if you need. Make it a bit faster for you."

Raedrick let out a little sigh of relief before he realized what he was doing. "I would very much appreciate that, thanks."

"Like I said, happy to help." Avery looked back at his son. "Watch the stove. I'll get the Constable set up." He moved to step out, then paused and looked back, pointed his index finger at

Jac. "Keep your nose out of that book. If you burn the bread again..."

He left the rest unsaid, but Jac bobbed his head quickly in acknowledgement then backed hurriedly back into the cabin.

Avery turned back to Raedrick and grinned at him. "Gotta keep boys on a tight leash, eh Constable?"

"I wouldn't know. My first is on the way any day now."

Avery did laugh then. "Well you'll find out soon enough." He reached out and gave Raedrick a companionable clap on the shoulder. "Come on."

Even using the cart that Avery and his son lent them, it took a long time to reach the gates of Melton's Ranch. Raedrick looked up at the sun, well past its zenith now and heading toward the mountain peaks on the eastern side of the Vale, and grimaced. Little chance they would get back before nightfall at this rate.

But there was no help for it. He needed answers, and quickly.

The gates to the ranch weren't gates per se. Just a wooden archway above two large, driven posts that looked to be hewn trunks from the local pine trees, spaced about fifteen feet apart. The arch was gracefully carved, almost looking like intertwining tree branches that were cradling the circled M that was Melton's brand. The entire structure was stained reddish-brown, to offset the lighter brown of the beaten path that flowed beneath it from the docks to the ranch buildings themselves another quarter mile or so ahead.

The largest of the buildings, Melton's house no doubt, stood above the others a short ways up the flank of the looming northern peak of the Hook. It was hewn from logs and had a front porch running the length of the house before large windows that would allow the owner to easily survey his domain.

Another, simpler building, no doubt for the ranch hands, lay off to the left. Long and narrow, single-storied, it had the same peaked roof as Melton's house but much smaller windows. It was painted off-white and had a single door that allowed entrance at the end of its long side closest to the path.

The ranch's stables were off to the right, smaller than the ranch hands' housing but more stoutly constructed from the look of it. Out-buildings and a larger structure that had the look of a mess hall were directly in front of them as they drove up.

The entire setup made a sort of open courtyard, almost. And in the center of that courtyard was a raised platform, almost like a reviewing stand except it was circular, with steps leading up to it at cardinal points around, and in its center was a tall pole, which had a quartet of iron rings fastened at head level on it. From the top of the pole flapped a white banner with a blue circled M.

Melton took himself seriously, it seemed.

There was a half dozen men clustered in front of the pole as Raedrick and company rode up. One of them stood on the raised planks of the platform, the rest were on the ground in front of him. The man on the platform was saying something, but he stopped when Raedrick pulled Avery's draft horse to a halt.

The speaking man narrowed his eyes at them, and the rest of the group turned to take their measure.

Raedrick nodded greeting. "Good afternoon, gentlemen," he said, and stepped down from the driver's seat. He hit the dirt and squatted for a moment, to remove the kinks from his legs, then he straightened and walked toward the group.

"I'm Raedrick Baletier, Constable of Lydelton. These are Hiram and Gilroy, my deputies."

Which wasn't strictly speaking true in the most formal sense, but they were acting in the role, so might as well give them the weight of the office. Especially since these people had never met any of them before.

And if there were shenanigans going on here...

The man atop the platform blinked, then grinned broadly. He stepped down and hurried across to meet Raedrick. As he did, Raedrick was struck by his brown eyes and the shape of his nose. He looked like -

"Glad to meet you, Constable. I'm Frederick Melton," the man said, and extended his hand.

Of course, he was Melton's son. As Raedrick clasped hands with him, he noted the circled-M stitched into the breast of his blue tunic, and the lack of that same insignia on the tunics of the men with him. Guess only family got to wear the brand.

"We got your note," Melton said, and Raedrick froze midway into starting to say why he had come.

Note? What note?

"And your man," said one of the men in the group in front of the platform.

"I'm sorry, what?" Raedrick said.

"The note you sent. Kurt!"

The man who had spoken from among the group stepped up next to Melton and pulled a piece of parchment out of his pocket. He held it out to Raedrick. He took it, and found his hands want to tremble as he read it.

Master Melton,

There is a man encamped in a lodge on the northern flank of the Hook's mountain. This man is a fugitive from justice, wanted for capital murder. Please take whatever action is necessary to apprehend him, in the name of the law.

Then followed a vivid description of Pat Holcomb. It was signed with Raedrick's name, and the handwriting looked a lot like his. But obviously it was not, because he for certain did <u>not</u> write this letter.

"Where did you get this?"

Melton and Kurt exchanged confused glances. "Your man delivered it yesterday afternoon," Melton said. "I sent Kurt and Ramo to the lodge, and they found him. Just like you said. Brought him back last night."

Raedrick swallowed. Hard. "You knew about the lodge?"

Melton shrugged. "No big secret. The yokels who built it let us know so we wouldn't be surprised to see them."

"Then Pat is here."

"Well kind of," Melton said. "He broke loose just before dawn and we had to...take steps."

Raedrick was already reeling from the letter. Now a sliver of dread ran up his spine. "What do you mean?"

"Come and see."

Melton turned and walked toward the stables. Kurt followed him, but paused to gesture for another of the men at the platform.

"Come on, Ramo," Kurt said.

The man he gestured toward bobbed his head and hurried to follow along as well.

Raedrick paused and looked back at Hiram and Gilroy. They looked as perplexed as he felt.

"Be ready for anything," Raedrick said.

They nodded. Gilroy loosened his sword in its scabbard, and Hiram took a moment to unlimber and string his bow.

Then the three of them turned and followed Melton and his men. As they went, Raedrick distinctly felt the weight of the remaining men's stares on his back.

He followed the Melton trio around to the stables' wide double doors, which were standing open, then went within.

It was dim inside, the only light coming from the open doors and some windows that were up in the rafters. But it was easy to see the various stalls and their equestrian guests. The smell of hay and manure filled the place, and struck Raedrick like a wave as he entered the place.

But he almost didn't notice, from the sight that greeted him immediately ahead, in the middle of the open area in front of the doors.

The man was hanging by the neck from a rope that had been strung up over one of the rafters, and was tied off to a post down near the ground. He was obviously dead. His hands were tied behind his back and his body swung back and forth slowly in the dim light.

His head was lolled forward, but Raedrick didn't need to see it; the bald head and grey fishing man's cloak told plainly who this was.

Melton looked from Pat's hanging body to Raedrick and grinned. "Sorry we couldn't deliver him to you. But justice is done, right?"

He reached out to clap Raedrick on the shoulder.

Raedrick reacted without thinking; the sight of Pat in that state drove all thought from him. Just a cold fury remained.

He swung his arm around and grabbed Melton's wrist before his hand could strike him, then he pivoted his waist and pulled.

Melton let out a surprised yelp, then tumbled to the ground, face first.

Raedrick yanked his arm upward, and Melton's yelp turned from surprised to pained. He knelt down, planting his knee into Melton's back.

"I did not write that letter," Raedrick growled.

"Wha - " Melton began, but Raedrick cut him off.

"You and your men are under arrest for murder."

Behind him, he heard Kurt and Ramo cry out with chagrin,

and begin to move. Then he heard the sound of steel drawing across leather and of a bowstring being drawn back.

He looked back to see Hiram standing between him and the two ranchers, his sword out in a guard, tip pointing at Kurt's throat. Gilroy had his bowstring back to his ear, but he wasn't aiming at the two of them; his point of aim was out the stable, where the other three hands had followed, and looked to be about to charge as well.

Or they would have, but they were frozen in place, eyeing Gilroy with confusion and fear on their faces.

"You're making a mistake, Constable," Melton said from beneath him. The initial shock and pain was gone from his voice; now there was just anger.

"Well it won't be the first time," Racdrick said, and gave another jerk on his arm. Then he reached with his free hand to the back of his belt, where he kept a set of manacles. "Cut him down, Hiram, then bind these other two."

He shifted his gaze back to the three men outside the stable. "These men are under arrest. Do not interfere." He used his best Squad Leader voice, and he could see it had the intended effect, because they collectively swallowed and took a half step back.

Gilroy glanced back at him, and Raedrick met his gaze for a moment. The fishing man nodded and turned his full attention back to the men outside.

Then Raedrick put the manacles on Melton and stood, rounding on Kurt and Ramo.

The two ranch hands' eyes followed Pat's body as Hiram lowered it to the ground. Then they looked at Raedrick with a mixture of chagrin, confusion, and fear. He returned their gaze with his battlefield command look.

After a second, whatever fight may have been in them left, and they lowered their eyes to the ground.

16

LAND HO

The sun was well set and the moon halfway up to its zenith above the western mountains when Heather docked at Horace's spot on the western-most of Lydelton's finger piers. Raedrick, of course, had nothing to do with it and didn't even bother to offer to help. The two fishing men went about the business of getting the boat tied down and equipment stowed with an efficiency that he could never match. In moments, the three of them, plus the Melton men, were off the boat and onto the dock.

There they paused. Raedrick looked back onto Heather's deck, where Pat's body still lay covered in the tarp that Gilroy had placed over it when they got underway from the Melton docks.

This whole situation stunk, and it was only going to get worse. Once Brice learned what had happened, and that Raedrick had arrested his son...

And what if the son was acting on orders from the father?

Raedrick shook his head, willing that thought down. Brice Melton was many things, but rashly violent to the point of murder? He couldn't believe that.

Still...

"You two bring these three to the Constabulary and lock them up. Then fetch the Healer's Circle and the priests to see to Pat's body."

Hiram nodded, but shot him a questioning look. "What are you going to do?" He sounded cautiously worried.

Raedrick flashed him a quick grin that he hoped was reassuring. Then he inhaled and straightened himself, squaring his shoulders. "I'm going to talk to the Mayor," he said, glancing up at the angle of the moon. He might have to wake Brimly up, at this hour. But there was no help for it; no way this could wait until morning.

"That should be fun," Gilroy said, in a tone that said he expected it to be anything but.

Raedrick snorted. "Keep a watch in the Constabulary. I don't want any trouble from them," he gestured toward Frederick, "or anyone else." He took a step away, then looked back at them. "And keep yourselves armed."

The two fishing men exchanged glances with each other, then nodded. Hiram nudged Frederick to get him moving. The young man complied. He still looked angry, and the gaze he shot Raedrick would set fire to a bundle of sticks at twelve paces. But beneath that anger he showed resignation, or at least he wasn't outwardly resisting anymore.

No doubt he expected his father to get him out of this, and quickly.

Wrong.

Raedrick turned away and moved quickly from the docks to dry land, and as he did so he felt a lightening in his step. Like somehow having dirt beneath his feet made up for some source of tension or other.

It wasn't that he didn't like boats. Far from it. But...

Whatever, he had work to get to and an unpleasant conversation to navigate. Or really two of them. The Mayor would probably be upset over what had happened.

Melton would be furious.

"Yeah, this is going to be real fun," he said to himself.

17

DEBRIEFING

Mayor Brimly's house lay on the west side of Lydelton, along the shore of the lake past the finger piers. Two stories tall and expansively broad, it was obviously the fruit of great business success. And Brimly had certainly achieved that before becoming Mayor.

Raedrick was unsure whether Brimly had always lived here or decided to settle down here after he retired from his business. It had never come up, and he had always assumed the former. But as he approached the house it suddenly gnawed at him that he didn't know for certain.

Whatever. He was just distracting himself from the sure to be unpleasant conversation that lay ahead. Bad enough that he would probably be waking the man -

But no, the windows were lit, both upstairs and down. The Mayor and his wife were still up and about, it seemed, so that was one concern taken care of.

He stepped up the three flagstone stairs to the Mayor's front door and reached for the pull bell to announce himself. But before he could pull it, the door opened.

"...three doses each day, and be very careful of the measurement. If - "

Master Sebastini stopped in mid-sentence as he saw Raedrick standing outside the door. He blinked, and glanced aside to his left, where the Mayor was standing in his shirtsleeves. Both men's expressions shifted, almost in unison, form earnest seriousness to surprise to chagrin to trepidation to wariness in the span of a few heartbeats.

Silence lingered for those few heartbeats, and it seemed to Raedrick that the silence carried a weight of its own. And then the Mayor cleared his throat slightly and nodded greeting.

"Constable. Didn't expect to see you so late."

Raedrick returned the nod, carefully giving the Mayor his full attention. Clearly something was going on with him and the Healer's Circle, and just as clearly it was something Brimly wasn't comfortable having him interrupt. Done was done, but no need to draw further attention to it.

"I've just come back from the Hook. I wouldn't have bothered you but there are some things you need to know about that can't wait til morning."

Brimly nodded slowly, his expression turning darker as he took in the import of Raedrick's words. "Well you'd better come in, then." He paused, looking aside at Sebastini. "Thank you, Ravi. I'll be in touch in the morning."

Sebastini inclined his head in concurrence. Then, with a quick, polite, "Good evening, Master Mayor," he stepped out.

Raedrick moved aside to let the older man pass, and Sebastini flashed him a gentle smile of thanks.

When he had gone, Brimly gestured for Raedrick to follow him, then he turned and walked further inside.

The interior of the Mayor's house was opulent, but not ostentatious. The first floor was dominated by a single large room that had a dining setting off to the left and a wall filled with stuffed bookshelves to the right. Ahead, a quartet of stuffed chairs sat around a smaller circular table, past which large double doors gave easy access to the lake at the house's rear. It was pleasantly cool from the broad windows at the back of the room, which were open to admit a breeze from off the lake, and there was the odor of spices of some sort on the air.

Mistress Brimly kept a tidy and pleasant house. Normally. But as Raedrick followed the Mayor toward the stuffed chairs he noticed a few things awry. Clutter where there hadn't been on previous visits. A dirty bowl and spoon on the dining table. One of the Mayor's jackets flung over a chair.

Something was definitely going on here, and Raedrick couldn't help feeling a sense of concern as he moved into the chair that the Mayor offered him.

"Well," Brimly said as he also moved to sit. "What is - "

A thump from upstairs, of something falling and hitting the floor, interrupted him. Followed by what sounded like a low moan, and then, plaintive and weak, but also demanding, "Wil!"

It was Mistress Brimly's voice, and it jerked the Mayor back to his full height. Chagrin followed swiftly by concern crossed his face, and he spared Raedrick just a glance before hurrying toward the stairwell. "A moment, Constable," he said, peremptorily.

Then he was gone, swift footsteps giving report of his progress--rapid progress--upstairs and across the space above Raedrick, into the bedroom he assumed. His voice and his wife's filtered down from upstairs but Raedrick couldn't make out exact words. Just tone, and the feeling of it.

His: concerned, caring. Hers: scared, confused, drowsy.

The worry Raedrick had felt earlier grew more intense, and he had to fight the impulse to head upstairs himself, and assist.

But he strongly suspected the Mayor would not take kindly to that intrusion into whatever this situation was. So he forced his instinct down and instead looked out at the moonlight reflecting off the softly lapping waves of the lake, clearly visible through the open windows.

It really was a great view. Very peaceful and calming. If circumstances were different, Raedrick could see how a man could waste hours just sitting looking out at it. And not have those hours be a waste at all.

Some minutes later, Brimly's footsteps announced his descent, and he came back into the great room. His expression was haggard, like whatever just happened had drained him. He swept past the stuffed chairs where Raedrick sat, not saying a word, and went over to the dining setting. Off to the side of the main table, a cabinet of red-stained wood sat up against the wall. An oblong crystal decanter, halfway filled with what looked to be whiskey--and good whiskey too, from what Raedrick had seen of the Mayor's taste--sat atop the cabinet.

Brimly opened one of the doors to the cabinet and withdrew a short, bulbous glass. He paused, looking back at Raedrick as though seeing him for the first time. "Would you like a drink, Raedrick?"

He shook his head. "No, thank you."

Brimly nodded then closed the cabinet door and poured himself a rather healthy portion from the decanter. Then he came back and settled into the chair he had been about to take before the ruckus from upstairs interrupted him.

He took a long sip from his glass then placed it down onto the table between them. "I should explain that," he said, making a quick, almost dismissive gesture upwards.

"There's no need.'

"Yes," Brimly said. "Yes there is." He drew in a breath, as though to steel himself, then looked Raedrick in the eye with as earnest, serious an expression as he had ever seen on the Mayor's face.

"Martha's been having...spells. Started a couple months ago. Mild at first, but they've been getting worse. Ravi tells me it's a degenerative disease of some sort, and..." His words caught in his throat and Brimly looked away, toward the windows and the lake. "She doesn't have much time left. Maybe a few months."

He reached for his glass again, and Raedrick rocked back as the import of the Mayor's words hit him. He didn't know Mistress Brimly very well, but she was kind, gentle, and steady. He had secretly thought her a bit of an anchor for the Mayor's occasionally flighty behavior.

He thought of his Lani, even now most likely helping her mother close up The Oarlock for the night despite how far along with child she was. The thought of losing her was something he didn't want to consider at all. But it would be one thing for her to go suddenly. To know it's coming, to watch its approach and be powerless to stop it...

He shuddered inwardly, and his heart went out to Brimly.

The Mayor took another drink from his whiskey and looked back at Raedrick. His eyes were wet. "That's why I'm not standing for re-election. I'm going to make her as comfortable as I can in the time she has left. And I can't do that as Mayor."

Raedrick nodded understanding. He opened his mouth to reply, but the Mayor continued before he could get a word out.

"Though after what happened tonight..."

Raedrick blinked. "What do you mean?"

Brimly cocked an eyebrow, but after a second he nodded. "Right. You weren't here. Melton kept to his word, made his pitch quick and pithy. Not a bad plan, if you ask me. Don't know how most of the people will go for it, though. Saw a lot of doubting faces in the crowd."

"Ok..." Raedrick let the word draw out into a question.

"But when Stepan got up to give his talk, he didn't get halfway through it when some woman from one of the farmsteads on the south side of the lake pushed forward. She's even greater with child than Lani, if you can believe it." Brimly raised an eyebrow at him and Raedrick frowned. "This woman--Telli--accused Stepan of being the father, and running out on her."

"What?"

Brimly nodded. "Stepan denied it. But his wife didn't seem to believe him. The whole thing collapsed into the two women haranguing him, and then nearly getting into a fistfight with each other." He shook his head and rolled his eyes toward the ceiling, as though asking the gods for mercy. "So he never got to finish his pitch and the entire meeting became a calamity."

"That is...." Raedrick stopped, unsure what to even say. That it was shocking would be an understatement. But also... "She's from the south side, you say? Melton's place?"

The Mayor cocked an eyebrow at him, suspicion darkening his features as he saw what Raedrick was getting at. After a moment, he shook his head. "No, the McAlister compound. Or at least, that's what someone told me. I'd never seen the woman before tonight."

That'd didn't necessarily rule out chicanery. The McAlister's were close enough to the Melton Ranch that they must have a relationship of some sort. But did he really think Melton would pull something like that?

"This was certainly good for Brice," Brimly said, echoing Raedrick's thoughts. "But I doubt he would have anything to do with it. Too convenient, and he's not that sort of underhanded."

Which didn't mean the Mayor thought he wasn't under-handed at all, Raedrick noted.

"Well that's moot now, anyway," Raedrick said.

Brimly looked at him sharply. "What do you mean?"

Raedrick took a breath, then told him the events of the day. The Mayor's expression grew successively darker as each second of the telling passed, and by the end he wore a deep scowl. "Tell me you aren't kidding about this."

"Master Mayor, I wouldn't - "

Brimly waved off the statement with a dismissing gesture. "I know. I know. Just, it's..." He shook his head. "Damn." Then he downed the rest of his whiskey in one swift swallow. "You know what this means, don't you?"

Raedrick had a pretty good idea, but he kept quiet to let the Mayor speak.

"It means Lydelton's going to end up being led by that popinjay Federson. No one's going to vote for Brice or Stepan after this." He threw up his hands and looked up at the ceiling, in the direction of his wife. "I'm going to have to step back in. That fool will run this town into the ground."

"I don't know that - "

The Mayor snorted an interruption. "Yes, you do." He sighed, then stood from his chair. "Young Melton and his men are in cells, yes?"

Raedrick nodded, also moving to stand.

"I'd better go talk with Brice. It'll be better if he hears about it from me." Brimly walked over to where his jacket lay. With a roll of his shoulders, he slipped it on and took a moment to button it up. "But you know, when the fishing men hear about this, they'll be out for payback. Mind you ensure nothing happens to them before the trial."

"I'm setting up a watch in the Constabulary. Just in case."

Brimly harrumphed softly, then nodded and turned toward his door.

Raedrick glanced upward, toward where Mistress Brimly presumably lay in bed. "What about - ?" He gestured toward the stairs when Brimly looked back at him.

Some of the resolve to action left the Mayor as he followed Raedrick's gesture with his eyes. "Ravi gave her something to help her sleep. Hadn't taken full effect before, but she's sleeping sound now, and will til morning." He fixed Raedrick with a look both serious and appealing. "I would appreciate it if you wouldn't spread word about her condition around. Like to keep this as private as we can, for as long as we can."

"Of course."

Brimly nodded again and inhaled, drawing himself up and putting his resolve back on. "Let's go."

18

PATERNAL VISITS

To say Brice Melton was displeased was to say that a thunderstorm brings a little bit of rain.

Entire chasms filled his face from the scowl he was wearing when he burst into Raedrick's office half an hour later. It didn't help that his hair was mussed and his shirt partly untucked. Brimly must have caught him in bed, or preparing for it, and he hadn't bothered to put on his jacket or make himself more presentable.

Raedrick couldn't blame him for that; wasn't often one's son ended up in a cell accused of murder. But still it was surprising; part of the image Melton had clearly worked to build up was as a man of control, and stature.

Funny how quickly that flew away. Or maybe not.

Raedrick decided to take the first watch in his office, sending Hiram and Gilroy home to get some rest. Gilroy would return in three hours, but in the meantime Raedrick had determined to get some work done.

He was seated at his desk when Melton arrived, writing notes on the day's events and getting a start on the report he would have to file with the judge, and with Marshall Leminster down in Mangin City. Since Lydelton's judge wasn't empowered to hear capital cases, Frederick, Kurt, and Ramo would have to be transferred there for trial, which meant the Royal Marshalls would have to come get him.

Leminster tended to come up once of twice a year anyway, but coordinating the transfer meant there could be a bit of a delay before the proceedings could come to a full resolution. So the sooner Leminster got the word, the better.

All the same, writing reports was one of Raedrick's least favorite things about this job.

So when the door practically burst off its hinges and Melton stormed in, he for a second felt a sense of relief, to be able to get away from the report for a while. Then the man's expression fully sank in as the father's angry gaze settled on Raedrick, and that brief elation faded a bit.

"Where's my son?" Melton said, without preamble or greeting.

Raedrick leaned back in his chair slightly and gestured toward the iron-barred door in the center of the rear wall of the Constabulary's front office. "Second cell on the left," he said.

Melton stalked forward and pulled the cell block door open--Raedrick had kept it unlocked since he was in the office. Then without another look in his direction, Melton went to see his son.

The door to the cell block was just iron bars; no real barrier at all. So unless someone went to the effort to be quiet it was usually easy to hear conversations taking place back there.

Melton made no effort to be quiet.

"Stupid boy! What did you think you were doing!?"

Raedrick winced at the tone--derisive, angry, and pained all at the same time. Frederick wasn't exactly a "boy" anymore. If he had less than twenty years Raedrick would be shocked. But it was clear the elder Melton--at least when he was angry--did not see his son as a man, and certainly not as an equal.

He turned his attention toward the report he was writing, willing himself not to listen as the younger Melton responded in a tone that made Raedrick think of a dog with its tail tucked, slinking back on his haunches in the face of a larger, more aggressive animal.

He might as well not have, because Brice just laid into him before he could get two words out. "I'm running for Mayor, you know that! Do you have nay idea what your stupidity has done to my campaign?"

"Father I - "

"I don't want to hear it!" Melton drew in a long, loud breath. Then he continued in a more measured tone, "I will take care of this. Keep your mouth shut and don't cause any more problems until then. We'll have a lot of work to do to clear up this mess."

Silence for a few seconds. Raedrick could imagine the expression on Frederick's face. Probably shame, probably chagrin. But he had to imagine disbelief would be there as well, for the apparent lack of concern about anything other than the Mayoral campaign.

Raedrick knew he was feeling that, himself.

"Do you understand?" Melton's voice was back to its normal calm, but his tone was hard as stone, brooking no objection.

More silence, but Raedrick could see the younger man's defeated nod in his mind's eye.

"Good." Footsteps, and then a moment later the elder Melton stepped back through the cell block door into the officer. He came over in front of Raedrick's desk and focused in on him.

"I assume you heard most of that."

Raedrick straightened in his chair and shrugged. "Kind of hard to miss it."

Melton looked back at the cell block door and sighed,

shaking his head. "Children can be trying." He flashed a small smile Raedrick's way, and just like that the mask of anger he had been wearing when he confronted his son faded away. "As you'll find out soon enough. Now." He gave Raedrick his full attention, his voice going into full business mode. "If you'll release him to me, I assure you there will be no further trouble from him."

Raedrick knew it was coming, but nevertheless the brashness of the man took him aback for a second. He put his pen down on his desk blotter and straightened in his chair before answering. "You know I can't do that. He killed a man."

Melton sniffed. "He brought a murderer to justice. Not the same thing."

"Pat wasn't proven to be a murderer." Melton opened his mouth to reply but Raedrick ran over him. "But even if he was, that's a matter for the law, not some random person to take into his own hands."

Melton's lips compressed. "I get it. You're sore that he stepped on your territory. Well maybe if you'd been more effective at your job, he wouldn't have had to. The way I see it - "

"There is no place for vigilante justice here, Master Melton. Not anymore, if ever there was. He and his fellows killed a man without trial. He confessed it to my face, and he will be tried for it."

"You can't be serious." Melton sounded dumbfounded, but beneath that amazement, a new anger was brewing, beginning to show through in his tone even as his expression tightened all the more.

"Completely."

Melton glowered, and for a second Raedrick thought he was going to try to take physical action. But instead he straightened, scowling. "We'll see what the Mayor and the Judge has to say about this." He turned to leave, his shoulders tight with pent up anger as he stalked toward the door.

But if he thought the Mayor would order Raedrick to release his son and his compatriots, or that the judge would, he was about to be sorely disappointed. Of that, Raedrick had no doubt.

Still...

"One more thing, Master Melton."

Melton paused in the process of opening the front door and looked back at him over his shoulder.

"When I was down at your ranch, I noticed a post in the center of the courtyard. Kind of post we used in the Army to flog prisoners. It had iron circlets driven in at just about the right height as well."

Melton's face shifted subtly, the anger remaining but now joined by something else....wariness?

"Your point, Constable?"

"When we spoke before you mentioned...chastisements. It's true that I have been neglecting you and yours these last months. I intend to change that, and if I find you or your people crossed a line..." He let the sentence drift into unspoken threat.

Melton's eyebrow quirked upward and he put on an approximation of a reassuring grin. The burning anger in his eyes put the lie to it, though.

"I of course welcome the long arm of the law to my land, Constable. I assure you, you'll find nothing amiss."

"Glad to hear it. Good night, Master Melton."

Melton gave a curt nod in return, then departed. The door closed loudly behind him.

Raedrick leaned back in his chair and had to suppress a groan. This whole situation was already ugly enough. But he had the feeling it was going to get a whole lot uglier.

19

CONFERENCE

The sun was up. He could tell that through his cracked-open eyelids. But Raedrick's body screamed at him that it was way, way too early for him to be moving.

Groaning, he turned away from the shake that had roused him, rolling onto his side and pulling his blanket tighter about himself. Way too early.

The shake came again, and the voice that was too beautiful for him to ignore.

"Raedrick, get up," Lani said, and he groaned again.

But he forced his eyes open and rolled up to a sitting position.

She was leaning over their bed--as much as she was able to, swollen as her belly was--looking at him with eyes that were apologetic beneath her neatly combed and braided blonde hair. Her sweet face looked much better rested than he felt, though there was worry in her eyes.

"The Mayor's called a meeting," she said. "Horace is downstairs to fetch you to it."

"Wonderful," he said, and forced his feet over the side of the bed onto the smooth wooden planks that made up their bedroom floor. He coughed, cleared his throat. "What's the hour?"

Lani stepped back and smoothed the dark blue dress she was wearing; it was larger to accommodate her belly, and had begun to rumple up a bit. "A couple hours before noon. I was just about to go in to help Mother with the lunchtime crowd."

Raedrick nodded, and rose. "I assume word got around about Melton's son and his men. Any trouble over it yet?"

Lani shrugged. "Not that I've heard. More people are interested in the Holiman fiasco, at least from the talk among the breakfast crowd."

Yes well, that figured. What was an arrest for murder compared with the drama of a love triangle, complete with jilted lover and bastard child? Still, Raedrick would have figured the fishing men would be upset about Pat.

Or maybe not. Just as likely many of them assumed Pat had been the one who killed Lester. And though he was more popular than Lester had been, if he had been the culprit it was hard to think he didn't get what was coming there.

Except for the whole law thing.

"Sounds like that was quite the drama."

Lani pursed her lips. "Yeah." There was something in the way she said it that made Raedrick stop donning his breaches and turn to look fully at her.

"What?"

"I don't know. It just seems awfully convenient. This woman shows up out of the blue, on the night Stepan was to give his speech?" She shook her head.

"That seems like the best possible time to get back at the man who ran out on you, if you ask me."

Lani nodded agreement, but her expression was still doubtful. "I suppose. But I've never seen her before, or even heard of her."

And she knew a wide cross-section of people from all over the Vale, and beyond, thanks to working the Oarlock with her mother.

"She probably only rarely came to town. The McAlister compound is pretty self-sufficient, from what I hear."

"Yeah. Well when would Stepan have gone down there to meet her then?" She shook her head again. "It doesn't add up. And I'm not the only one who thinks so. I heard at least a couple people talking that way at breakfast."

Raedrick pursed his lips, considering. She had a valid point. Stepan's smithy did good business. And yes, he had a couple of apprentices. But he was the master, the one who did the truly skillful parts of the work. He probably wouldn't have all that much spare time to go traipsing about.

Then again, it didn't take a lot of pondering to recall any number of men Raedrick had known or heard of who got themselves into similar, or worse, trouble with apparently no spare time to do so.

"Well, the truth will come out, one way or the other," he said as he pulled on a boot. "But for now, I'd better not keep the Mayor waiting."

Lani rolled her eyes slightly and then grinned broadly at him. "Have fun, dear."

Raedrick was still chuckling over that when he stepped outside their little house and found Horace, looking far less good humored, waiting for him.

"Heard you had a late night," Horace said by way of greeting as he turned to walk alongside Raedrick toward Main Street, and City Hall.

Raedrick grunted. "I suppose it shows."

"It does." Horace flashed him a quick approximation of a grin that didn't quite make it to his eyes, which were grim.

Raedrick couldn't blame him. "Your men heard the word?"

Horace nodded. "Don't mind telling you, only reason they haven't strung up young Frederick already is you have him." He paused, then added. "And some of them aren't sure Pat <u>didn't</u> kill Lester, and got what he had coming for it."

Well that was something, at least. "I'm keeping a watch at the Constabulary. If anyone thinks to cause trouble - "

"No worries about that, Constable," Horace said. "I've got it in hand."

"Alright." And it was. If Horace said he had it under control, it was good and solidly lashed down.

One worry at least that Raedrick could shed from his mind. It was getting crowded in there.

The mood was strangely, to Raedrick's mind, upbeat when he walked into the Mayor's office, Horace at his heels. Or at least the Mayor wore an almost cheerful expression, as did Tim Federson. The others' backs were to him, so Raedrick couldn't see. But he doubted they did.

Still, the Mayor's, "Good morning Constable," made it almost seem like a normal week. For a second.

"Apologies for being late," Raedrick said, and Brimly snorted.

"You had a late night." He cleared his throat. "Now then. With the murder of Lester resolved, we need to decide how we're to proceed for the rest of this campaign."

Raedrick blinked. "I'm not sure it's been resolved, Mayor."

Melton snorted now, turning around in his chair to look at Raedrick with a baleful expression on his face. "It is plain to see."

Of course, he would want it to be. Pat's guilt was the lynchpin to showing his son was innocent.

Raedrick shook his head. "The timing doesn't work for Pat to have been the culprit."

Brimly cocked his head at him. "That's not what you said last night."

"I didn't say anything last night. But I had time to think it through on watch after we met." He held up his index finger. "The dockmaster's son at the Hook said he saw a group of men going from the area of the lodge to the Melton ranch a bit before midnight." He raised a second finger. "If Pat killed Lester, he would have had to have gotten a horse and raced from here to there in three hours, maybe four? Without killing or laming the horse in the dark." He shook his head. "Can't be done. He had to have left before Lester was killed."

Glances all around between the other men in the room. Melton's expression grew darker. Tim almost looked stricken. Horace appeared surprised, then relieved, then puzzled. Stepan just looked glum.

"But why would he have left?" Horace said. "He told everyone he was getting some rack time before Melton's speech that night. He seemed pretty excited to be there for it." He raised an eyebrow at Melton and grinned slightly. "I think he had a trick of some sort up his sleeve for you."

"He certainly did," Melton said. "Murder." He looked away from Horace back toward the Mayor. "Maybe he had an ally do it. Or maybe -"

"If that is the case, the ally is still at large," Raedrick said. "So no, it's not resolved yet."

Whatever hint of a good mood had been in the office when Raedrick arrived faded.

Mayor Brimly was frowning deeply. "I have to agree with Horace though, Raedrick. Pat would not have just slipped away like that. Not during the campaign week at all, especially not just before his strongest competitor's speech." He paused, blinked, then flushed and looked first at Stepan then Tim. "Meaning no offense of course, gentlemen."

If anything, Tim looked amused by the Mayor's lapse. He

made a dismissive wave of his hand. Stepan glowered, but said nothing.

"Maybe he was taken against his will," Raedrick replied. "I don't know. Yet."

"Yes, well I'm sure you'll figure it all out. But for now, we have the campaign to finish," Melton said. "And I must be allowed to address the populace again."

The Mayor looked askance at him. "Why?"

"They need to know that what happened between Pat and my son was done without my knowledge or order."

Brimly shook his head. "No one thinks you were involved, Brice. If - "

"Yes they do. Some of my men have heard rumblings in the taprooms. I insist I be allowed to put this slander to bed."

"You've already had your allotted time. Unless Tim wants to give up some of - "

"No way," Tim said, looking daggers at Melton. "Bad enough he hedged in on Stepan's time yesterday. He wants to make another case, he can do it during the general question time tomorrow."

The Mayor nodded agreement. "I was just about to say that very thing." He looked back at Melton and raised and eyebrow. "Tomorrow is set aside for questions and answers from the populace. If it comes up, you can make your point then."

Melton glowered for a long moment, but then his shoulders slumped slightly and he nodded concession. "Very well. But I think it will be more powerful if it comes from Frederick's mouth, not mine."

Raedrick blinked hard, surprised at the ranch owner's gall. "I'm not hauling a prisoner out before the crowd to give a speech, or make a statement about the thing he's charged with."

"I agree," the Mayor said. "Until the trial we can't compel him to speak about it; that would basically be a public confession. No point in having a trial at all, after that."

Raedrick could tell Melton didn't like it, but also that he couldn't see a way to refute his and the Mayor's refusal. So he just shrugged, and looked away.

"Alright," Brimly said. "I believe everything is in readiness for this evening. Tim?"

Tim nodded. "Looking forward to it."

"In that case I think we're done here. Thank you gentlemen."

20

A CRY FOR HELP

*R*aedrick followed the others out of the Mayor's office. Melton wasted no time hurrying away down the stairs. Tim went quickly as well. But Stepan slowed and then stopped as he reached the landing of the stairs. He rested his hand on the darkly-stained pine guardrail that lined the stairwell, and seemed to ponder for a second. Then he straightened and turned around to look Raedrick in the eye.

"I need a word, Constable."

Raedrick traded a glance with Horace, who gave a little shrug before stepping around Stepan to descend the stairs, leaving he and Raedrick alone in the room.

"What can I do for you, Stepan?"

"You can help me clear my name, that's what."

Raedrick blinked. This was unexpected. Not that Stepan would want to disprove the allegations Telli had made, but -

"I'm not sure that's any of my business. There's no crime been committed, or alleged."

"Falsely accusing someone isn't a crime?"

"Is it false?"

Stepan's nostril's flared. His shoulders tensed and for a

second Raedrick almost thought the smith was going to lash out at him. "Damn right it is. I wouldn't have known that woman to pick her out of a crowd before last night."

"Alright. But I still -"

Stepan stepped closer, his eyes darting down the stairwell for a second. When he spoke, it was more quietly; clearly he didn't want his words to carry. "Come on, Raedrick. You can see what's going on as well as I."

Raedrick raised an eyebrow at him, and he rolled his eyes.

"Someone's trying to fix the election. I mean, first they try to frame up Pat, then they get this woman to attack me. Just you wait; something will happen with Tim tonight." He glanced back down the stairwell again, then he leaned forward, pitching his voice even lower. "It's Melton. I'm telling you!"

That didn't make any sense. "If Melton is running a grand conspiracy, he's doing a bad job of it. I've got his son locked up for murder. That's not how you fix a campaign in your favor."

Stepan waved his hand to dismiss Raedrick's words. "An unexpected twist; something he didn't plan on." His eyes narrowed, and he added, "But you know Frederick isn't his only son. And I've heard there is friction between them. So maybe..." He trailed off, raising an eyebrow.

"You aren't ever going to convince me that Melton set his own son up to commit murder, and then be arrested for it."

"That's not what I mean. But if there is bad blood between them, maybe this is a happy coincidence for him."

Stepan was grasping at straws on that one. No way was Melton's anger and embarrassment last night feigned. Sure, he'd probably been up scheming half the night on how to spin it to his advantage, but to think he was somehow, someway pleased by what had befallen his son...

Raedrick shook his head. No way.

Stepan looked at him in silence for a moment, then his face

dropped. The anger, the affront he felt over the accusation was still there, but that flew away, replaced by a dejection that suffused his entire body. His shoulders slumped and he lowered his gaze to the floor.

"I slept in the smithy last night. My wife won't let me in the house. Over something I did. Not. Do!" He inhaled through his nose and his voice broke, almost as though he was about to break down completely.

"Stepan, I - "

He looked back up into Raedrick's eyes, and Raedrick stopped mid-word. The appeal was plain; the desperation.

Raedrick swallowed, then nodded. "Alright. I'll look into it. But I can't promise anything."

Stepan nodded. "That's all I ask."

He reached out and clapped Raedrick on the shoulder. Even in his dejected state, the power of it almost set Raedrick back a step. Stepan kept his gaze locked onto Raedrick's for a moment.

Then he turned and clumped down the stairs.

Raedrick watched him go, and sighed.

21

LUNCH PLANS

The lunch crowd at The Oarlock was larger than usual, and Raedrick noted a number of faces he didn't recognize as he entered and strode to his normal place at the end of the bar.

The new faces belonged to mostly younger men, who had the look of fellows who were used to physical labor. They were scattered around in groups of three or four at the various tables, dressed in simple but apparently well-made shirts and trousers.

As he came in, many of those faces turned to look at him. He felt their gazes on them as he moved through the room, and the hairs on the back of his neck stood up.

Lani was behind the bar with Rolf; her mother was probably back in the kitchens chivvying the cook staff as they worked to fill orders. She had on a white apron over the blue dress she'd donned earlier, and had a set-upon look about her as he settled onto his seat, like it had been a busy morning.

She came over to him and slid a tankard across the bar top. It smelled of mulling spices, and the good wine that Molli kept in stock from a vineyard off to the east of Mangin City. He accepted it with a grateful smile and took a moment to inhale the aroma before taking a sip.

"How was the meeting with the Mayor?"

The tingle of the spices warmed his throat as he swallowed, then he shrugged and set the tankard back down. "About as expected." He glanced to the right, toward one of the closest tables of strangers. They had ceased obviously watching him, but still...

"Big crowd."

Lani followed his gaze with her eyes and her expression darkened slightly. "Melton's men. They've been filtering in all morning."

Raedrick cocked an eyebrow at her, and she made a little shrug.

"They've not been causing any trouble, if that's what you're wondering. But..." She let the sentence die, but he got what she was getting at.

The group at the Melton Ranch had not been happy with him when he took Frederick and the other two away. And certainly they wouldn't be feeling any better about things this morning; especially considering what their boss probably had to say about it.

At the same time, it was campaign season, and as citizens of the Vale they had every right to participate in the process.

"Did this many of them come up for the last campaign?"

She shook her head. "A few. But most folks from the outlying farms didn't bother before."

And if they were going to come up at all, it made sense they'd come for their boss' speech, and for the final day of voting.

Wonderful.

Raedrick shook his head and took another, longer sip from his tankard. "I wish Julian was here."

Lani looked at him with eyes that were suddenly softer. She reached out and laid her hand over his. "I miss him too."

Raedrick rolled his hand over to take hold of hers, then gave it a gentle squeeze. "He's better at thinking around twists and turns than I am."

Her right eyebrow rose. "Oh, that's all, is it?"

He made a little shrug, and felt the corners of his mouth rising; she could see right through him, he knew. But it was still warming and amusing when she showed it.

A clatter off to the left broke the moment. He whipped his head around and saw one of the serving girls standing by the row of tables along the wall opposite the bar, a look of chagrin and embarrassment on her face, and the platters of food that had been on her tray scattered and shattered on the floor at her feet.

Someone a few tables away began clapping, and the poor girl's cheeks flushed hot red as her embarrassment grew even deeper.

"Oh bother," Lani said softly. She moved as though to hurry over to help clean up the mess, but the other two serving girls on duty beat her to it. In moments, the three of them were busily scooping up the detritus. So instead, she looked at Rolf and said, "Better send word to the kitchen to redo that table's order."

Rolf rolled his eyes in consternation but nodded, then he ambled over to the end of the bar and the swinging doors back to the kitchens.

Lani looked back at Raedrick and sighed. "It's always something, right?"

Raedrick nodded. "That's what I was just thinking when I came in, and why I miss Julian's deviousness."

Both eyebrows rose at him.

"Stepan asked me to clear his name. How am I supposed to do that? I don't know this Telli woman or how to find her, and anyway how do you prove that he's not the father, assuming he's telling the truth?"

Lani pursed her lips and considered. "Well I can tell you where she is." He blinked, and she rolled her eyes. "I told you people were talking about it at breakfast, remember?"

"She's staying here?"

Lani shook her head. "No, over at Helen Sheridan's. But one of Helen's daughters was in earlier, and that got the conversation going."

Raedrick knew Helen. She was a widow with a house on the east side of town. Since her children were all grown, with families of their own, she would let out some of her rooms to travelers during caravan season for extra income. Raedrick had only been by her place a couple times, but it was neat and well-kept. Charming, even. And Helen herself still retained enough of her youthful beauty that Raedrick was certain she had been stunning, once upon a time. And she had the grace and kind wit to go with it.

He nodded. "Guess I'd better go over to Helen's, then."

Lani just looked at him for a long moment. Then she shook her head.

"What?"

She sighed. "Raedrick, you're the constable. You go over there asking questions from her...it looks like an inquisition."

"No it doesn't. I - "

"She's a young woman about to give birth without a husband. Who just accused a Mayoral candidate of running out on her. She's scared, under tremendous pressure. And then in walks the law, looking for her."

Raedrick hadn't thought about it that way. He found he couldn't refute Lani's words. All the same... "This morning you said you didn't believe her."

"I said I was suspicious. Not the same thing."

"Ok. So what - ?"

"Leave it to me."

Raedrick coughed. "Excuse me?"

Lani chuckled softly. "This requires a woman's touch."

"Lani, you're in no condition to be exerting yourself. If - " The level gaze she sent his way stopped the words cold. He paused, cleared his throat, then tried a different tack. "Why not one of the other girls?"

"I'm in the same condition she is. Except for the unwed part." She patted her belly--and had it swollen a bit more since just this morning?--and smiled warmly at him. "She'll appreciate being able to commiserate with someone who understands." That right eyebrow rose again. "Trust me."

Raedrick found himself grinning back at her. "And I thought Julian was the devious one."

Lani laughed.

22

QUESTIONING

Gilroy was on duty in the Constabulary when Raedrick walked in. He was sitting behind Julian's desk, his feet propped up on the desk and reading a small leather-bound book.

His eyes left the pages, then widened slightly when he saw Raedrick. For a second he looked to tense--like part of him wanted to jerk his feet down--but then he grinned and nodded. "Constable."

Raedrick chose not to mention the feet on the desk. "How are our guests?"

The fishing man shrugged. "Pretty quiet since lunch. The little one was complaining up a storm earlier, about how unfair this is and they were just trying to help you out, do as you asked them. Melton shut him up, but it took a while."

Raedrick raised and eyebrow at that. "Frederick?"

Gilroy nodded, looking amused. It seemed the young Melton had been learning some prudence after all. Or his father had put him straight. Either way, it was an interesting development.

Kind of.

Right that minute though, Raedrick would have preferred

him to be a bit less prudent. He strode over to his desk and opened the top drawer, where had his notes and the beginning of the case report for this event stored. And the supposed letter from himself that had set Frederick and his compatriots off to grab, and hang, Pat.

He held the letter up and read it through again. For about the hundredth time.

Had to give whomever had created it credit; the signature at the bottom was close to his. Close enough to pass a quick inspection, at least.

He fished out one of his previous reports and flicked to the back page, and his signature, then compared the Melton letter with that genuine article side by side.

Yes. Quite close.

That meant the forger had access to or seen paperwork that Raedrick had personally signed, and practiced, at least a little. Which didn't exactly lower the pool of potential culprits down very far. Raedrick had occasion to post notices to the public from time to time. The notices went up in public places, and he signed all of them.

And come to think on it, he had never considered or paid attention to what happened to those notices after they became dated or otherwise moot. Not like he had gathered them up after they were of no more use.

Why would he?

That left the pool of potential culprits huge. So he would have to figure out the culprit's identity the old fashioned way.

Sighing, he straightened and, forged letter still in hand, turned toward the cell block door. "I'm going to have a word with them," he said to Gilroy, who nodded, then went back to his book.

The three men were lying on their cots in their respective cells when Raedrick entered the cell block. The lighting was dim, provided only by the access from the front office and by a pair of oil lamps mounted above the entrance door and at the end of the lines of cells, and by narrow slit windows at the back of each cell, well above eye level. But there was enough light to see the men clearly enough.

There had been a murmured conversation going on; Raedrick heard soft voices as he swung the door open to come in. But it ceased as he approached, and he saw three heads rising off of rough pillows to regard him.

He stopped in front of Frederick Melton's cell, and the ranch heir took his time to stretch languidly before sitting up on his cot to face him.

"Here to let us out, Constable?" Melton said, bitter sarcasm in his tone.

"Not just yet," Raedrick said. He carefully kept his tone neutral, professional. He'd seen during their journey back from the Hook yesterday that Frederick would try to needle him. No need to play along with it. "Wanted to talk about this." He held up the forged note.

"What's to say? Told you all of it yesterday."

"Tell me more about the man that delivered it."

"Didn't see him." Melton looked to his left. "Kurt?"

The man in the cell next to him didn't sit up. He just shrugged from his position lying on his cot. "Pretty average guy. Couple fingers shorter than you, Constable. Sandy brown hair. Round face. Clothes looked like homespun wool. I met him out by the road from the docks about an hour before sunset. He said he'd been sent by you to spread the word about a fugitive." He waved a hand toward the letter. "There you have it."

The wheels were turning fast in Raedrick's head. "Before sunset you say?"

Kurt nodded.

"Was he on foot, or - ?"

"No. Rode a dun mare. Soon as he delivered the note, he cantered back north, like he had business back in town."

That clinched it. The attack on Lester had not even happened yet--or at best it was just occurring--at the time the messenger, whoever he was, delivered the letter. Which meant he, or someone he was working with, knew it was coming.

That made two conspirators, working together. If not more.

Raedrick chewed on that for a moment. "Had you ever seen the man before or since?"

"Nope."

"Did he have an accent, or anything?"

"Just sounded like someone lived in a town all his life."

Raedrick nodded. It was something to go on, at least. "Thank you, gentlemen."

He turned to go, but stopped when Melton spoke up. "You're not really going to keep us locked up over this are you? We were suckers in this one; thought we were doing your work."

Raedrick looked over his shoulder and scowled at him. "You still killed a man."

Melton's sullen return stare spoke volumes.

When Raedrick returned to the front office, Gilroy was still nose in his book. He perked up a bit more quickly when Raedrick closed the door behind himself, though.

"They say anything useful?"

"Could be. When's Hiram getting here?"

"A couple hours." Gilroy grinned at him. "Figured you'd want the watch turned over before the speeches tonight."

Raedrick nodded. "We're going to need to be on the lookout. Whoever's behind this may try to pull something." He sat down at his desk and pulled out a piece of paper. Unstoppering the bottle of ink on his desk, he commenced to writing down the description of the man Kurt had given him. In moments he had two copies of the description written down.

"When Hiram gets here, show him this," he said as he finished. "If anyone looking like this fellow comes around here while we're at the speech, he is to put the man in irons and throw him in a cell."

Standing, he walked over to Gilroy and handed one of the pages to him. Gilroy scanned it and raised a questioning eyebrow. "That fits about half the town, Constable."

Raedrick shrugged. "It's the best description we have. I'm going to go see Clarice and see if she saw this man and Lester together at all, then I need to talk to Horace."

"Gonna borrow more of the men, huh?"

"Not much choice." He turned for the door. "I'll meet you at Town Hall half hour before the speeches."

"Honor to serve."

Despite the complete lack of humor in Gilroy's tone, Raedrick still had to chuckle at that.

23

SCHOOL TIME

Helena's school was in the same small building it had been for years, just off Main Street tucked between a larger residence and one of the Covington Brothers' store houses. It was a single story, with the same sharply angled roof that all of Lydelton's structures had. Within was a larger front room where the classes were held and a smaller office space in the rear.

When Raedrick entered, the place was empty of pupils. Not unusual for this time of year, or so he understood. As harvest time and the end of caravan season approached, children had more duties to attend to around their homes to prepare for the winter, so Helena and her sister had scaled back on classes to accommodate. And Helena maintained that tradition now.

From what he'd heard, kids rarely stayed past lunch these days.

Still, he was unsurprised to find Helena and Clarice hard at work in the office space in the rear. No pupils didn't mean nothing to do, after all.

The front classroom area was mostly open, with a collection of smaller kid-sized desks and chairs off to the left in front of a board of black slate that was mounted on the wall, a craft area off to the right with easels, jars of paint, and various wood tools, and a small library directly ahead as one walked in the front door. By contrast, the office was all clutter. Two desks pushed together in the center of the room so the pair of them could sit and face each other, a cork board on the wall adjacent to the desks on which all manner of planning documents were pegged. More bookshelves behind the desk to the right, and a wall-full of file cabinets behind the desk to the left.

The women were seated at the desks when Raedrick walked in. Helena, to the right, was pointing at a document that she apparently had slid across to Clarice's desk with the nub of a pen.

"...No, you can see right here. It's - " Helena stopped when she saw Raedrick and flushed slightly. "Constable. Good to see you again."

Clarice seemed to flinch slightly as Helena spoke. But she put on a welcoming half-smile when she turned to look at Raedrick.

"Pardon, ladies," he said. "I see you're busy but I wonder if I could have another word with Clarice?"

Clarice swallowed slightly. "About Lester and Pat? I told you all I know."

"This will be quick," Raedrick said. He stepped toward her desk and held the paper with the description of the man who had met with Kurt out to her. "I think this man is involved with everything that's been going on."

"What do you mean?" Helena said. "I thought you arrested the men who killed Pat?"

Raderick looked at her and nodded.

"So what else is there?"

"I don't believe Pat killed Lester." He looked from Helena back to Clarice. "This man set the Meltons onto Pat's trail. So he had to know something about what happened. Have you seen him before, maybe hanging around Pat or Lester at some point?"

Clarice's hand trembled slightly as she reached out for the paper. Her eyes had a haunted look as her fingers closed, and no wonder what with all she'd been through lately. And now to have him tell her this worst part may not be over after all...

She scanned the page, and pursed her lips for a moment before shaking her head and handing it back to him. "I don't know, Constable. Don't think so." A brief pause, then she added, "But I could be wrong. I mean, that sounds like a lot of people around here."

The near echo of Gilroy's words from a few minutes ago did not help, true though it may be.

"Well, think on it. If you can remember anything at all, it could help."

"May I?" Helena said, and Raedrick passed the page over to her.

After a moment's reading, Helena looked up and over at Clarice, then chuckled. "You know, this sounds a bit like your cousin Sid."

Clarice's return look was not amused. "And half the other men around here." She scowled, then shook her head vigorously. "Besides, Sid's short and wouldn't know how to ride a horse if it walked up and kicked him." Her scowl faded as she looked back at Raedrick, slowly turning into a sheepish half-grin. "Which actually did happen one time, Constable. He's been afraid of horses ever since."

"Yes, well, I don't think cousin Sid needs to be worried over much." He took the page back from Helena and folded it, then stuck it in his pocket. "Again, think on it and let me know if you remember anything. No matter how small."

The two women nodded, and Raedrick turned to walk out.

But before he could reach the little school's front door, it burst open, flying back on its hinges until it smashed into the front room's inner wall with a loud crunching bang. A young man, darker of skin than most people in the Vale with loosely-flowing black hair that reached his shoulders and wearing the white and yellow of the Healer's Circle, rushed in. His yellow-brown eyes were wide and he had a look of anxious intensity on his face.

Raedrick recognized him immediately: William, Ravi Sebastini's apprentice.

"Constable, thank the gods you're still here. Come quickly. There's been an incident."

Raedrick raised a calming hand toward him. "Slow down. What's going on?"

"There was a fight at the Sheridan guest house. A woman's been badly injured. Master Sebastini sent me to find you, and your office said you were here."

A little sliver of dread crept up Raedrick's spine. The Sheridan house? That's where Lani was going to question Telli. If -

The worry must have shown on his face, because William blanched, then shook his head vigorously. "Not your wife, but she was pretty shaken up over it."

"Over what? What the hell happened?"

William spread his hands helplessly, and Raedrick forced the concern that was turning into irritation down. No need to harangue William for what he probably didn't know. Instead he nodded. "Alright, let's go."

24

____

BRAWLING

he Healer's Circle was located a couple blocks east of Raedrick's office, on the north side of town. Small, almost nondescript in its simple single-story construction, it had a long porch that took up the entire front of the building and a set of hitching posts, and a simple sign reading "Healer's Circle" up near the peak of the building's sharply-angled roof.

When Raedrick and William arrived, a small crowd, half a dozen strong, was milling about in front of the building. Mostly women except for one older fellow with frizzy grey hair and a long, bulbous nose who wore the grey cloak of a fishing man. Raedrick recognized him--Tom, one of the eldest in the guild and the best navigator on the Lake. Or so his reputation said.

The women were mostly unknown to him, but they were all about Lani's age. Three of them were clearly well along in pregnancy and if Raedrick had to guess the other two were not far behind; just not showing as much.

Raedrick knew Lani met with a group of women who were in a family way once or twice a week to give each other support and pass on wisdom that their sex had learned over the centuries about childbirth. He had never attended, of course, but he presumed this must be the group.

And now that he thought on it, it would make sense that they would meet at the Healer's Circle. No doubt Master Sebastini's guild would have wisdom to share with them as well.

Or not? Come to think on it, midwives weren't part of the Healer's Circle, so...

He brought his wandering thoughts into order as the group turned toward him. The women all wore expressions merging from deeply concerned to outright angry. Tom looked to be in a towering rage.

"You need to lock that Holiman woman up, Constable," Tom said by way of greeting.

Raedrick stopped for a second, the abruptness of the statement, and the anger with which it was said, catching him by surprise.

"What?"

Tom glowered at him, but before he could reply the young woman standing next to him in a blue dress with white trim spoke up. She was a few inches shorter than Lani and pretty with wavy brown hair. And a nose that was not quite as pronounced at Tom's, but close enough that he presumed they must be family.

She was also very far along, almost as ready to let her child loose as Lani.

"Lani sent me a note and asked me to go with her to talk with Telli. I had just finished up having lunch with Grandpa, so he came also."

"Alright..."

"We were just sitting down, the three of us--me, Lani, and Telli--in Helen's parlor when Linsy stormed in, screaming at the poor girl."

Poor girl. Interesting way to refer to a home wrecker.

Raedrick shoved that thought down, hard. If her accusation was true, Stepan had as much a hand in that travesty as she did.

"I was waiting outside," Tom broke in. He sniffed. "Not wanting to intrude on women's business, you know? Anyway, along comes Linsy stalking down the street with a face like a storm cloud and leaving a trail of dust behind her like the ground itself was scared of her passing. Didn't realize what she was up to until she was past me, and then..." He shook his head.

Tom's granddaughter continued, "She lit into her again and again. At first Telli just took it, but then Linsy called her a whore and she got up out of her seat. And then Linsy just leapt on her. They were wrestling and fighting... Lani tried to pull them apart but she got shoved and fell back into the wall and hit her head."

That sliver of dread shot back up Raedrick's spine. "Is she - ?"

From beside him, William put in, "She's fine from what I could tell before Master Sebastini sent me for you."

"But Telli ain't," the young woman said. "Linsy did...something...while they were scrabbling, and then Telli fell headfirst. The corner of the table got her right in..." She trailed off, her hands going reflexively to her belly, and Raedrick winced.

Tom waited a second, then said, "I got in there to find Elsbet trying to help Telli and Linsy just standing there. Like she was happy she mighta killed the girl's kid." His face was already a mask of anger; it somehow darkened even more. "I got Lani on her feet then helped Elsbet get Telli moving, and we all came here."

"And where is Linsy now?"

Elsbet nodded toward the building. "Inside, with them."

Raedrick sighed and shook his head. "Alright." When it rains, it pours, it seemed. "Thanks Tom. Elsbet. I will need to take formal statements from you later, but you don't need to hang around here if you -"

"I ain't going anywhere, Constable," Elsbet said.

"Up to you." He eyed her more closely. She was angry, yes, but there was something more there than her grandfather's obvious moral outrage. "Are you friends with Telli, or - ?"

She shook her head. "Not as you'd say friends, but..." Again her hands strayed to her expanding belly. "I can relate to what she's going through."

Well yes, of course she could. She was pregnant as well. But...from the expression on her face as she said that, there was something more there. Raedrick found himself wondering who the father of her child was. He didn't know Elsbet--hadn't really interacted with her before today--but as he thought of it he wasn't sure if he had heard whether she was married or not.

From the looks the other women were giving her right then-- there was pity there, and on one face, a bit of scorn--he suspected the answer was no.

That would explain how she could feel a bond with Telli, he supposed.

He nodded in understanding, then turned and waved his hand for William to lead the way. "Lead on, William," he said. "Let's see if we can sort this out."

William looked doubtful.

25

PROGNOSIS

he foyer of the Healer's Circle was simply adorned, but comfortable. Tapestries on the walls depicted anonymous members of the Circle engaged in their duties aiding the sick and injured in a variety of locales. There were cushioned seats, colored in the white and yellow of the Circle, lining both walls to left and right beneath the tapestries, and a long, narrow table holding a crystal decanter filled with water, and half a dozen glasses for clients' use, stood in the center. The door to the rear treatment rooms was directly across from the main entrance, and was closed.

The two women in the room could not have been more different. Lani, all blonde and pretty and big in the belly from their child, sat in one of the chairs to the right in the same dress she had on earlier, and with a bandage wrapped around her forehead and right temple.

Opposite her, and decidedly not looking in her direction was Linsy Holiman. Raedrick didn't know her all that well, though they had met and interacted several times in the last year. She was older and had a matronly look. Grey streaked her short-cut black hair, and while Lani was normally slender Linsy was more plump about the middle and her bosom strained the laces of the green blouse she was wearing over a brown-grey skirt. Her expression was hard to read; stony at first glance, except for her eyes, which simmered with something...anger? Guilt? Both, or neither?

When Raedrick followed William inside, Linsy's eyes flicked away from where they had been fixed on the door to the treatment rooms toward him, and she blanched and looked quickly away from him back toward the door. Her cheeks flushed slightly, but her lips remained clamped shut.

Lani perked up noticeably and made to stand up, but he waved her back down into her chair before she could.

"Take it easy," he said, slipping into the chair next to her. "Are you alight?"

She nodded. "Just a bump on the head and a little cut. No big deal." She glanced over toward Linsy and added, more loudly as though to make certain she heard, "It was an accident."

Raedrick looked at her askance, and she shrugged. "It was. Linsy didn't mean it to happen."

Across the way, Linsy glanced back at Lani and her cheeks flushed a bit more deeply. Raedrick just looked at her while William walked around the table in the center of the room and stepped through the doorway to the treatment rooms. Only after the door closed behind him did Raedrick stand and move over toward Linsy.

"Is that right, Mistress Holiman? Was all this an accident?"

She visibly avoided looking at him for a long couple of seconds, but when she finally did he saw that the confusion of emotions he had first observed on her face had just grown deeper. Her lips trembled and she worked her jaw, clearly struggling over whether to speak, or what to say if she did. Tears were welling up in her eyes, as yet unshed.

After a moment, she shook her head, but whether as a negative or as a refusal to speak Raedrick would not hazard to guess.

The treatment room door opened then, breaking some of the tension that had built up as Master Sebastini came out. He quickly took in the scene, then zeroed in on Raedrick and nodded.

"Ah, Constable. Good," he said, and came over to stand in front of Raedrick. His lined face was businesslike, but grim, and his eyes were tight with concern. "I've been in with young Telli. She has a contusion to her belly, just to the right of her navel. A deep bruise; painful but not life-threatening in and of itself."

Raedrick heard Lani draw in a relieved breath, but Sebastini made a quick shake of his head.

"Were she not with child, that is. The baby appears to be in a fair amount of distress, and she has begun contracting. Her water broke and there is bleeding." Sebastini's eyebrows rose meaningfully.

Raedrick didn't know that much about the birthing process in humans, except that it was probably not that dissimilar to what he'd seen with horses in the past. But it was a time when husbands were intently kept away by their wives, the midwives, and really every woman in the vicinity. No need for him to make things harder on the woman giving birth, he'd heard them say.

But little knowledge or no, Sebastini's description didn't sound good at all.

Sebastini nodded at the expression Raedrick must have been making. "I have sent for the midwife to get her opinion, but I believe the situation is dire. The baby's life is in danger, and perhaps Telli's as well. Her body wasn't ready for labor just yet, and so..." He spread his hands helplessly. "She may be able to deliver naturally. But if not, I will have to take steps. And even then the child may not live."

His eyes flicked toward Linsy, who seemed to be shrinking in on herself now. "Thought you should know, in case you need to take any action."

Raedrick nodded, turning to look at Linsy more fully. "I think that can wait until we see how the situation turns out, Master Sebastini."

"Well that is your business, of course," Sebastini said. He glanced at Linsy again and sniffed, then turned his attention fully back to Raedrick. "All that said, young Telli is in good hands. Mistress Kampari has assisted in hundreds of deliveries over the years, and I have performed a dozen or more sections."

"I have no doubt about your skill, Master Sebastini. Do you need anything?"

He shook his head. "Just room to work."

Raedrick nodded. "Please send word to my office when the situation is resolved, either way."

"It may take hours; perhaps not until the morning. You know how labor can go."

"That's fine." He fixed Linsy with a level look. "We will await word there."

Linsy met his gaze, and gathered herself visibly. "No. That is, I would rather - "

"We will await word <u>there</u>," Raedrick said again, putting on the command tone he'd learned in the Army.

Linsy looked to protest again, but after a second lowered her gaze and nodded grudging acceptance.

"Very well," Sebastini said. "I will keep you informed, Constable."

"Thank you."

Raedrick saw that Lani had stood and was moving over to Linsy's side. She reached out and placed her hand on the other woman's shoulder, and she flinched. But after a second, Linsy looked back up and met Lani's gaze. Soundless communication passed between them somehow, then Lani nodded, a gentle expression on her face. Linsy took hold of her hand and gave it a gentle squeeze, gratitude in her eyes.

Raedrick wasn't sure he'd be as forgiving were he in Lani's position. But then, he supposed there were reasons he had decided to marry her, and beautiful as she was that wasn't the main one.

"Let's go," he said. Then waited while Lani helped Linsy to her feet. Then he strode to the door, to lead his latest prisoner to his office, and the cell block.

26

HOLDING PATTERN

"Is this really necessary, Constable?"

Stepan Holiman looked like a man beaten down by a century of woes, despite his only having experienced less than half that many years. He stood before Raedrick's desk, hands clasped in front of his belly like a boy pleading with his father, and Raedrick's heart couldn't help going out to the man.

He had gone through a lot the last two days.

He must have thought he was on top of the world, or at least of the Mayoral race, after Lester's killing had disrupted Pat's candidacy. He could not have believed that Brice Melton would be more popular than him, or Pat.

Or at least, Raedrick couldn't believe that. And for good reason.

And personal ones.

But then, for Telli's accusation to come out in public, and his wife to believe it so he couldn't even sleep at home...

And now, for his wife to stand accused of assault and perhaps the murder of Telli, or of her baby... That must be weighing the man down beyond anything Raedrick could consider.

Still...

Raedrick dropped his pen into its inkwell and leaned back in his chair, giving Stepan his most level gaze. "It is. At the least, she is guilty of assault. At most..." He shook his head. "Until I learn how Telli and her baby fare from Master Sebastini, it's the cell for her."

"But..." Stepan spluttered, looking like he really wanted to object. But after a few seconds, he nodded, and lowered his gaze to the floor. He inhaled deeply, then sighed. "Can I see her, at least?"

Raedrick nodded. "Of course." He stood and walked around his desk, and around Stepan, to the barred door leading back into the cell block.

The keys were hanging on a hook next to the door, like they always did when the office was manned. A lesser man than Stepan--really than any of the men who lived in Lydelton--might have tried to grab the key away and make his own entry. And if he had, Raedrick could not have really blamed him, though he would have had to force him not too, and then charge him for it.

But he hadn't, and Raedrick was thankful for that for a heartbeat, and then he felt guilty for having doubted the man even for that small amount of time.

Silly.

He opened the cell block door, then waited for Stepan to enter and followed after him.

Raedrick, and Julian when he was in town, didn't have cause to lock up women nearly as often as men. Oh, they caused mischief just as often, but more often it was non-violent mischief, the type that could be handled without having to resort to physical restraint.

Still, it did happen, and so they had a cell set up to accommodate a woman's different needs. The first cell on the right as one walked into the block. It had curtains hung up inside the cell's barred walls, so that the woman in question could draw them closed when she needed privacy from the eyes of any men who might also be shut up in the block with her.

They were drab, originally died midnight blue but now going to grey. But they were better than nothing.

Linsy had the side curtains on the side of her cell drawn all the way to the front, but those at the front open, so she could see out at something besides the narrow slit of the window at the back of her cell.

But also not see the trio of men shut up across from her.

Stepan walked over to stand in front of her cell, and she scowled. "What are you doing here?"

"I could ask you the same thing, Linsy. What were you thinking?"

She looked away, toward the wall adjoining the front office, and said nothing.

Stepan sighed and looked back at Raedrick. "Give us a minute, please."

Raedrick nodded, and stepped back into the front room. Hiram was sitting at Julian's desk now, having relived Gilroy while Raedrick had been away. He had a wry expression on his face.

"Seems you're locking up people associated with <u>all</u> the candidates," he said, and glanced back toward the cell block door.

Raedrick grunted and closed the door. "Hopefully not." He didn't want to think about what might happen this evening during Tim's speech. "But if I have to..." He shook his head and went back to his desk. The seat felt harder than it usually did as he sat back down upon it.

Through the bars of the cell block, Stepan's voice carried clearly. "I told you, I had nothing to do with her. Why won't you believe me?"

The silence in response to his plea carried entire levels of anger and scorn.

To avoid listening to the lack of real conversation, Raedrick said, "I haven't had a chance to talk to Horace yet. Have you seen him?"

Hiram shrugged. "Just in passing. It's been a heavy catch today from what I hear, so he's been busy at the docks. But I think Gilroy's going to tap him for you."

Raedrick nodded. "Good. We're going to need all the help we can get, if we're to find the guy behind all this." And the heavy catch was not going to make getting that help any easier.

"Gilroy told me. But you know, I'm not sure I see a grand conspiracy here. Maybe this guy had it in for Pat, but that doesn't mean he made Stepan lie with that Telli. And can you blame Linsy for going after her?"

Raedrick gave him a level look, but had to admit Hiram had a point. Maybe Stepan really <u>had</u> done it. And no, he couldn't blame Linsy for being affronted. Still... "Doesn't give her leave to do what she did."

Hiram shrugged.

A few moments of relative silence from the cell block later, punctuated only by Stepan's futile attempts to engage his wife in conversation, the cell block door opened and Stepan came back into the front office. He looked, if possible, even more set upon than when he came in. And that was saying something.

There were bags under his eyes, like he hadn't slept, and his hair was disheveled. His clothes were rumpled, and he moved in a manner that was far different from his normal upright, confident gait. His shoulders were slumped and his eyes downcast, his expression one of utmost misery.

Stepan paused, looking back into the cell block and his estranged wife, then closed the door slowly. He just stood there for a long several seconds. Then he drew a breath and turned back to Raedrick.

"How long will she have to stay here?"

"Until Master Leminster sends word, one way or the other. Might be til morning, he said."

Stepan nodded. His jaw worked, like he was chewing on something. Then he raised his head fully and pulled himself erect. "I'd like to stay here with her until then."

Raedrick could understand his sentiment, but he shook his head in the negative. "I understand that. But we don't have any beds here, and I won't have someone sleeping on the floor. This is an office of the law." And not a flophouse, he didn't say.

"Then I'll stay in the cell next to hers."

"Stepan, Hiram and I need to leave for Tim's speech in a half hour. I'll have to lock the cell block and take the key when we do that. And you need to be there, also."

Stepan shook his head vigorously. "No, I need to be here, with her. To hell with the election, otherwise."

Behind Stepan's back, Hiram raised his eyebrows.

Raedrick just looked at Stepan for a moment, considering. There really was no harm in granting the man's request. Against normal protocol, but not against any law or rule. Just not entirely proper.

But then, what <u>was</u> proper this week? It was like the entire town had been flipped on its head, with everything that had been going on. And, he had to admit he would insist on the same thing if it were Lani in the cell, whatever the circumstances that had put her there.

Finally, he nodded. "Very well. I'll send word to the Oarlock to make up five evening meals instead of four. You'll have to pay for yours." His budget covered food for prisoners, which Stepan was not.

"Of course."

"But," Raedrick said, putting his stern squad leader tone into his voice and pointing an index finger at Stepan, "You're not to engage with the Melton men at all. And if Linsy doesn't want to talk, you will not push it. I won't tolerate any trouble in there. Do you understand?"

Stepan blinked, then his face took on a look of affront for a moment. But he quickly relaxed, and nodded acquiescence.

"The cell should be unlocked. Make yourself at home."

Stepan flashed the tiniest hint of an ironic smile, that didn't even come close to breaking the look of misery on his face. He nodded again and pulled the cell block door open, then stepped back inside.

Icy silence greeted him, followed by something from one of the Melton men that Raedrick couldn't quite make out, though the mocking tone carried its meaning clear as day.

Raedrick watched the blacksmith's retreating back as he vanished from sight within the cell block, and pondered for a moment. Then he shook his head at the convoluted nastiness of all of this.

"You don't want me to stay here during the speech?" Hiram sounded surprised.

Raedrick looked back at him and shook his head. "The man Kurt described might be there. I want every eye we can muster in the crowd in case he is. And," he pushed down a shudder, "if something bad does happen, I'll need every hand as well."

"Lots of Melton men in town. You don't think they'll try to spring him?" Hiram gestured toward the cell block, and Frederick.

Raedrick shrugged. "I'll lock the front door as well. If they manage to get through that, the cell block door, and the cell doors they deserve to bust him out." He paused then added, "And it's not like we don't know where they'll be taking him if they do."

"Fair enough." Hiram shook his head, then let out a short half-laugh. "What sort of chicanery do you think lies in store for Tim tonight?"

"I hope to the gods nothing."

Hiram's expression told Raedrick he wouldn't take that bet.

Considering everything that had happened this week so far, Raedrick couldn't blame him.

27

SPECIAL DELIVERY

Raedrick couldn't believe it, but the evening, and his later night of sleep, had been uninterrupted.

Not a long night of sleep; he had taken the first watch back in the Constabulary after Tim Federson's speech and hadn't been relieved by Gilroy until four bells past midnight. But it was sleep nonetheless, and unspoiled by new trouble either during the speech or throughout the night.

He awoke with sunlight streaming in through the one narrow window in the bedchamber he shared with Lani and permitted himself a long, pleasant stretch in bed before he got up about the day. Then he got dressed and went to The Oarlock, where Lani was helping her mother with the last of the breakfast crowd.

Even as he enjoyed a sumptuous meal of eggs, toasted bread, and bacon with a flagon of mulled cider to wash it down, he had the feeling that surely something was going to rear its head and turn the day into a cavalcade of stress.

But nothing came.

Even the Melton men in the breakfast crowd seemed to not

be regarding him with anything but the normal attention one gives to any other person taking in the beginnings of his day.

At the office, Gilroy was at Julian's desk just as he had been when Raedrick left, though less informally than he had been yesterday. And sure enough, he reported no issues the entire night through.

Amazing, and more than Raedrick could have hoped considering the rest of the week previous.

He settled down into his desk chair and looked at the report he had begun writing to the judge about Linsy Holiman yesterday. It was complete except for the part about the charge he intended to lay against her. That still remained to be seen, and pondering that sent some of the good cheer that had been creeping into Raedrick's mind scampering away to the corners.

He frowned. "Any word from the Healer's Circle?"

Across the office, Gilroy shook his head, and Raedrick sighed. Not that he was surprised--deliveries take time. Still...

"Is Stepan still back there?" He gestured toward the cell block door.

Gilroy nodded. "Came out around dawn to check on his kids, he said. But he's in there now."

"No trouble with the two of them, or the Melton men?"

"Not that I've heard, no. Everyone was just crashed out when The Oarlock sent over prisoners breakfast. Mistress Holiman looked like she didn't sleep much though."

Again, hardly a surprise. She had to be bouncing between guilt over what she'd done to worry over the baby--because he couldn't believe she actually would wish harm on the child--to anger at Stepan to the gods only knew what other conflicting emotion. She'd had a rough couple of days.

Which didn't excuse the assault, even though it explained it.

"Well let's just hope today is a quiet one. If - "

Two quick raps on the front door interrupted him, and

Raedrick turned to see William step within. The Apprentice Healer didn't look at all like a man who had been up all night assisting with a troubled birthing. His hair was neatly combed, his Healers Circle robes pristinely clean and apparently freshly-pressed.

"We were just talking about you," Gilroy said by way of greeting, and William flashed a quick grin at him. Then he turned his gaze toward Raedrick.

"Master Sebastini thought you would be in at this hour. He requests that you come to the Guildhouse, and bring Master and Mistress Holiman with you."

"The delivery is done then?"

He nodded. "At three bells last night."

But that was hours ago, and Raedrick had been here in the office then! "And he only sent word now?" He couldn't help but let some frustration show through in his tone.

But William didn't notice, or if he did it didn't cause him to flinch. "The Master thought it would do you good to get a full night's sleep. And anyway neither the baby nor mother were in condition to receive visitors then."

Raedrick chewed on that for a moment, then nodded. Made sense, and he had to admit he appreciated Master Sebastini's consideration. "Both are well?"

"Tired. In need of recovery. But yes."

"Good. We'll be right along."

William stepped out, and Gilroy said, "You want me to stay here?"

Raedrick shook his head. "No. We'll lock the building up, but I'd like you along."

"Will do."

The front room in the Healer's Circle felt cramped with all the people gathered there: Raedrick, Gilroy, Stepan, Linsy, Master Sebastini, William, and Mistress Kampari, whom Raedrick had gotten to know quite a bit better over these last few months as Lani's pregnancy had progressed.

She was slight of build, coming barely to Raedrick's shoulder. Her skin, slightly darker than William's, was drawn tight around her face like she had been shrunk down onto herself, but while on some that might make them look shriveled or unsightly, it gave her a timeless appearance so Raedrick had never been able to guess her age.

She had been in the Vale serving as midwife for a couple decades now though, he knew. So he figured it was probably safest not to ask.

Her eyes were slightly-yellowish brown, and conveyed good humor and a quick mind, and she kept her hair in a cluster of braids that descended past her shoulders like the cowl of a cloak. Today, though, the good humor was gone from her eyes and she held a swaddled baby close to her bosom as the group from the Constabulary walked in.

Sebastini nodded greeting as everyone got settled around the table in the center of the room.

"Thank you for coming, Constable," Sebastini said. "As I believe William told you, we worked with young Telli until late last night. It was a difficult process, and and in the end I was forced to perform a section in order to birth the child safely." He smiled in satisfaction though, as he nodded and continued, "But Telli is well and resting, and the baby appears in fine health."

To his left, Stepan let out a relieved sigh, earning him a sharp look from Linsy, who stood separated from her husband by Gilroy. That look conveyed entire levels of accusation and disgust.

If he noted it, Stepan didn't respond, but the room seemed to grow several degrees colder to Raedrick's point of view.

Sebastini cleared his throat slightly, no doubt picking up on the rising tension. "It wouldn't have done either mother or child good to have company then, and I figured we all needed our rest, or I would have sent word earlier. But now," he gestured toward Mistress Kampari, "I thought you might like to meet the boy."

The midwife nodded and slowly, gently, lowered the infant onto the table. Then undid part of the swaddling so they could have a look at him.

A startled gasp from someone echoed Raedrick's surprise.

The child was dark. Almost as dark as William and Mistress Kampari.

Though he had promised to help Stepan clear his name, Raedrick hadn't been entirely certain that was even possible, because there was a good chance Telli had been telling the truth. But seeing the child -

"No way that's Stepan's kid," Gilroy said, finishing Raedrick's thought for him.

Raedrick shook his head in agreement. "No. No it's not."

He looked up and to his left, and saw Stepan staring at his wife. There was no accusation there, but there <u>was</u> a certain, "See, I told you so," to the look.

Linsy just stared at the baby for a long moment that stretched out into a short eternity. Then she looked up and met her husband's gaze. Her eyes welled up and her mouth flopped open and shut for a second. Then she gave a wordless cry and turned to flee toward the outside door.

Gilroy moved as though to grab her; she was technically a prisoner, after all. But Raedrick gave a quick shake of his head, and the fishing man let her go.

In a brief flash of light from outside, she was through the door, which closed behind her with a solid thunk.

Stepan stood rooted in place for a second. Then he glanced from Sebastini to Mistress Kampari to Raedrick and back. "Thank you," he said. Then he darted after his wife. "Linsy, wait," he shouted before he too was gone behind the solid weight of wood separating inside from out.

Silence loomed for a moment as Raedrick took a moment to fully process what had just happened. Then he gave Sebastini his Constable Means Business look. "I need to talk with Telli."

Sebastini nodded. "I thought you would. I gave her a sedative to help her rest but she should be coming around momentarily."

"Good."

"But Constable, whatever else she may have done, she is still my - " a clearing of the throat from Mistress Kampari brought an apologetic smile onto his face and a nod in her direction. "- is our patient. She is not ready to be moved from bed, and will not be for some days. I will not tolerate anything that could jeopardize or slow her recovery." The look he directed back at Raedrick put his Constable Means Business look to shame, and Raedrick found himself flushing slightly.

Ever so slightly.

"Of course. Just a polite conversation."

Sebastini nodded. "Then come with me."

28

REVELATIONS

*R*aedrick had been in this treatment room within the Healers Circle once before, nine months ago. When Jared Tolburt had shown up in the dead of Lydelton's winter. His arrival had almost cost Raedrick and Julian their lives--the second time Jared had done that--and upended the lives of several others in town, Master Sebastini included.

Now, as he stepped up to the side of that same bed, where Telli sat propped up on a stack of pillows as she pressed her newborn to her breast, he couldn't help but wonder if this visit wasn't going to upend things yet again.

If so, might have to ask Master Sebastini to convert the room to a different use.

Raedrick forced aside the half-chuckle that thought almost brought out. This wasn't a time for lighthearted fun. What Telli had done here was serious. Considering the other events that had taken place this week surrounding the campaign, it was deadly serious.

And she seemed to realize it. She didn't meet his gaze as he approached, just kept her eyes down toward the infant whose skin, so much darker than hers or Stepan's, had put the lie to her accusation.

She was out of her own clothes, wearing instead a plain white patient's gown that she had unlaced on the right side to let her son eat. Despite her downcast eyes, or perhaps because of them, the outfit and her pose gave her an aura of loving innocence. The kind of image a painter might like to produce to display motherhood in all its wonder.

Except for the deceit. However much he might find his heartstrings tugged a little, Raedrick couldn't set that aside.

"I think it's time for the truth, Telli," he said.

She didn't look up, just sighed and nodded. Her wavy black hair, which hung loosely around her face, bobbed slightly in time with her nod. "Holiman's not the father."

Master Sebastini, who stood on the opposite side of the bed from Raedrick, gave her a frank look. "We all came to that conclusion already, my dear."

"Who is?" Raedrick asked, willfully not using the gentle tone Sebastini had.

She drew a long breath, then finally looked up to meet his eyes. There was shame there, and he was glad to see remorse. But also defiance. "One of the drivers in the last caravan that came through last Fall had an accident. He couldn't continue on with them and the McAllisters let him winter over with them to heal. He left when the caravan came back through this Spring. But in between, we..." She left the rest of the thought dangle, but Raedrick didn't need the details. They were obvious.

She went on, "I didn't know I was..." she ran her finger gently down her son's face "...until well after he'd left. We'd kept it quiet so the McAllisters didn't know it was him. They assumed the father was a local and I didn't tell them otherwise."

"Why not?"

She shrugged. "His caravan comes through once or twice a

year. An outsider messing with a local girl and then leaving... Well, you know how some people can be. When he came back through..." She shook her head. "And anyway I wanted to tell him first, next I saw him."

"And when was that going to be?"

"When he left this Spring he said they should be coming again in the Fall. But earlier this summer a letter arrived. His caravan had its route shifted, and they were going to be using the southern passes from now on." Her voice caught in her throat. "We were never going to see each other again. I didn't even know how to get a letter to him; all he did was say goodbye. No mention of where he was going to be at all."

The destitution in her tone rang true to Raedrick, and he couldn't help feeling his heart go out to her. Bad enough to be a young woman who had lost her man. But to lose him after she learned she was pregnant, and with no prospect of even how to tell him about it... It was hard for unwed mothers under the best of circumstances; it would be crushing under the position she had found herself.

Which was not an excuse for how she had chosen to deal with it. He steeled himself, and pressed on.

"So you had to come up with another plan," Raedrick said.

She shook her head. "Not in the way you mean. When they found out I was with child, I thought the McAllisters would throw me out. But they surprised me. Mistress McAllister hugged me and said I could stay with them as long as I wanted. That they think of me almost as a daughter, and this would almost be another grandchild." Her voice did break then, and her eyes welled up.

She must have been thinking how that goodwill must be completely dashed now, or would be once the truth came out.

Again Raedrick felt his heart going out to her, but he

squashed that hard. "So why did you do it?" he asked, putting all the accusation into it that he could.

She flinched away, dislodging her son from his latch, and he let out a little cry of dissatisfaction. For a heartbeat, the look she gave Raedrick carried her own accusation. Then she lowered her gaze again and took a second to get the baby re-settled before answering.

"I was hanging laundry up to dry about two weeks ago when a man rode up to the compound. Never seen him before, but he knew who I was. Called me by name, and told me he knew about my problem and wanted to help."

The hairs on Raerick's neck stood up. "Who was he?"

Telli shook her head. "Like I said, never saw him before. His name was Simon, and he said he had good coin to pay if I did him a favor." She looked back at Raedrick and raised an eyebrow.

He didn't need to ask what the favor was. "How much?"

She shrugged. "Enough so I could get my own place, not have to live on the McAllisters' charity. They've been good to me, but I want more than that, you know?"

"So you were to show up, name Stepan, and then you'd get paid after the election."

She shook her head. "He gave me part of the money upfront. The rest afterwords."

Master Sebastini pursed his lips. "But you had to know as soon as the baby was born that the truth would come out. What was your plan for after?"

She snorted out a bitter half-laugh. "I wasn't due for another three weeks. Then it wouldn't matter. Simon would have the election turn out the way he wanted, and I would be on a caravan for Calas before the baby came. Except..." She gestured toward the once-more nursing boy; that said it all.

"And how did he want it to turn out?" Raedrick asked,

leaning forward a bit. The hackles on his neck were only standing up straighter now.

She shook her head. "He didn't say and I didn't ask. To be honest, Constable, no one outside of town cares who's the Mayor. Except Brice Melton, I guess. But I didn't even <u>think</u> to ask."

Raedrick shared a long look with Master Sebastini. The old healer looked at least as troubled as Raedrick felt. The fact that there was a conspiracy afoot to thwart the election was obvious by all that had gone on so far this week. But still Raedrick hadn't really wanted to believe it. It all could have just been coincidence.

No way that was possible now, after this revelation. He swallowed. Hard.

"When were you going to get paid out?"

"Soon as the results were certified. I'd meet him, he'd settle up with me, and then we'd go our separate ways."

Raedrick looked back at her and saw that remorse and shame was still there, but the defiance had increased a tad, as though confessing had stiffened her spine a bit.

"Meet him where?"

"A farmstead four markers up the road to Mangin City from the branch at the Eastflow."

Raedrick had been that way several times. There were a number of isolated farmsteads in that area, but... "There's nothing at that marker."

She shrugged. "He said it's a half-mile south from there. You can't see it from the road because of a hill."

Which Raedrick supposed was reasonable. He hadn't scouted out every farmstead in the Vale; he'd had no reason to. Yet. Still, her naiveté was showing. "Good thing for you Linsy has a temper. You wouldn't have gotten paid if you had made that meeting."

She frowned at him for a second, then her eyes went wide and she gasped in an inhalation. She shook her head in denial, and he just looked at her. She had to see it. No one who would put a scheme like this into motion would leave a loose end like her to possibly point back to him somehow.

She paled visibly, and began to tremble. Her arms reflexively tightened around her son, pressing him more firmly against her breast.

Raedrick leaned forward again, so that he would loom over her. "Describe this Simon to me."

She swallowed then, still trembling, nodded. "He was a little shorter than you. Decent-looking but not handsome. He had a round face with a little dimple in his right cheek, almost like a scar but not quite? Curly light brown hair. Brown eyes. He had money; enough to pay me and enough to own a horse, but he didn't dress fancy. Like the farmhands do."

A shiver went up Raedrick's spine. "What was he riding?"

She looked at him strangely for a second, then cocked her head, thinking. Finally, she shrugged. "A dun mare, I think."

Unless he was very much mistaken, Telli had just described the same man who had passed the forged letter to Kurt, Melton's man.

The shiver that had been growing, and threatening to turn his blood to ice, instead melted beneath an inferno of anger as the full import of that realization struck home. He nodded and took a step back. "Thank you, Telli."

Then he gestured for Sebastini to follow him, and he shoved his way through the treatment room door.

Telli said something behind him, but he didn't hear it.

When he reached the entrance room, Gilroy was chatting with Mistress Kampari about something, and sipping on a goblet of water from the visitor's carafe. Their eyes met, and Gilroy's widened slightly. He downed his water in a quick swallow and put the goblet down, Mistress Kampari forgotten, apparently.

"What's the word?"

Raedrick replied, "Rouse Hiram. The two of you arm yourselves, then meet me at The Oarlocks' stables in an hour. We're going on the hunt."

Gilory nodded, then turned on his heel and hurried from the building. Raedrick turned back to Sebastini and Mistress Kampari.

"I have to brief the Mayor. But until I tell you otherwise, no one gets in to see her except yourselves and William. If word reaches this Simon that the cat is out of the bag before we catch up with him..."

He didn't finish the sentence, and from the look on Sebastini's face, he didn't have to. The Healer nodded emphatically. "She will be safe here. See about your duty, Constable."

Raedrick returned the nod, then he followed Gilroy out into the sunlight.

29

FARMSTEAD

The sun was beginning its descent toward the mountains to Lydelton's east when Raedrick, Hiram, and Gilroy reined in at the fourth marker.

The markers here were roughly the same as those down by the Hook. They were placed at regular intervals to help measure distances along the roads, but almost more importantly they allowed a traveler to tell where the road even was during the winter months. Most of the time, anyway.

To say that snow was plentiful here was to call a river a trickle of water, and Raedrick had heard tell of winters years back where even the markers were completely submerged beneath the snow drifts.

For now at least, that wasn't an issue. The grass growing on the rolling hills to Lake Glimmermere's east was green going to the yellow of autumn, waving in the afternoon's gentle breeze. Against that backdrop, the markers were easily seen, even from a distance.

The fourth marker didn't look any different from the others, but it felt weightier somehow as Raedrick halted beside it.

"To the south from here she said?" Hiram asked.

The fishing man was on a white gelding that Molli Millens had loaned him from the stables. Gilroy's was spotted black and white, an older mare. Neither man looked particularly comfortable in the saddle; they spent most of their time on the boats, after all. But they also knew how to deal with an unstable surface beneath their feet, so they hadn't had too much difficulty.

Still, Raedrick had no doubt they would both be a bit sore in the morning.

He nodded. "I guess it's this hill here that we need to go around." The terrain rose steadily the further east one rode, gradually turning into the eastern flank of the Saddleback Mountains, with only Holbart's Pass allowing a reasonable way to travel in that direction. But some hills along the way stood out more than others, and the hill rising quickly to the south of the road here was among the larger in the vicinity.

Made sense Raedrick hadn't known there was a farmstead here. But again he kicked himself for not paying enough attention to the rest of the Vale outside of Lydelton's limits. Had he done that, the incident between Pat and Melton's men may not have ended the way it had, forged letter or no.

"Looks like someone's been through here a time or two," Gilroy said, gesturing toward the grass along the road a dozen or so yards farther along to the east.

And sure enough, some of that grass was bent over, as though someone had pushed through to the south. But not very recently, from the look of it.

Still, it was an indication that Telli's story was correct.

Raedrick clucked his horse forward, then turned down the little trail.

"You'd think if someone was living out here the track would be more well-used," Gilroy said after a minute or so of following it, echoing what Raedrick had been starting to think himself.

But then, a small self-sufficient farmstead might not need to come to town all that often. Or maybe they had taken a different route, intentionally not creating a guide to their place from the main road. Bandits were not unknown, even here.

And especially after the damage Isenholf's band had done a year and a half ago, when Raedrick and Julian had first come to town...

They rounded the flank of the southern hill, and Raedrick drew up short.

There was a farmstead here, all right.

The main house was built up against the rising hillside, made from hewn logs that must have been a real struggle to haul over from one of the scattered copses that littered the hill country. It looked to be no more than a single room, and as usual it had a steeply-peaked roof. Below the house on a relatively flat piece of land was a fenced-in area several hundred yards on a side that looked to have been tilled at some point. A small shed or shack stood off to the side of the planting area, where the farmer would have kept his tools.

Past the planting area and downslope a little ways the sunlight glinted off of something reflective; a small pond? It would explain why a farmer would have chosen to set up here.

It all looked like a nice little place where a small family could support itself and maybe make some extra money by selling their excess crops.

Except the side of the house nearest Raedrick was blackened and charred, the roof sagging in on itself. The field had certainly been tilled in the past, but now it was gone to weed and grass, only the linear lumps that the previous years' tilling had created in the soil giving away that previous work.

The fence was broken in two places, and broken pieces of what must have been furniture from inside the house was scattered around out front of the house's front door.

"Bugger me," Hiram said, and Gilroy grunted agreement.

Raedrick scowled, and nodded. "This happened a while ago. Must have been one of the farmsteads Isenholf burned out. Either of you know whose place this was?"

Head shakes from both fishing men, and Raedrick sighed.

There never had been a full count made of the families who had been displaced, or outright killed, by Isenholf's band of brigands. One reason was the lack of a recent census of the population outside of Lydelton proper. But beyond that, many of those who had been worst affected simply decided to leave.

Raedrick recalled seeing a fair number of families, or widowed wives or husbands, book passage with a caravan for Calas or Mangin City that summer after he and Julian first arrived. After going through Isenholf's depredations, they simply decided living in such an isolated area wasn't for them. Or they couldn't bear to be where they had lost loved ones.

Either way, he had known there were likely a lot of isolated farmsteads around the Vale that hadn't been rebuilt, because there was no one to rebuild them. At least for a while. The subsequent influx of new people in the year and a half since had probably seen some of those farmsteads rebuilt.

But clearly this one had not been.

"Damn shame," he said "But if Telli was supposed to meet Simon here, he may have left some sign. I'm going to check the house. You two have a look at the field and the shed."

Hiram and Gilroy nodded, and Raedrick nudged his horse to a walk.

He dismounted in front of the house's front door, next to what looked like a table leg that had been hewn in two.

There was a light breeze, and as he stood looking at the gaping doorway into that burned-out place he thought for a second he could smell char on that breeze.

Silly; whatever had happened here occurred well over a year

ago. It was just his imagination playing tricks on him. Squaring his shoulders, he clumped up the three steps leading to the house's front door and stepped within.

It was even worse that it looked from outside.

The roof wasn't just sagging, it had collapsed at the house's rear. Sunlight streamed in through half a dozen holes, lending illumination. Raedrick could see what looked like the remains of a bed for two beneath the collapsed roof section. And another, smaller bed off to the right, where the hottest of the flames had apparently burned. The bed--if that's what it was--was mostly burnt, and there were weeds growing up through broken gaps in the floorboards, nearly engulfing it.

But it looked child-sized.

Raedrick said a quick prayer that this hadn't happened at night; that the kid had been outside playing, and wasn't engulfed in the conflagration that had taken his house.

It was possible. Even probable.

He had a hard time convincing himself, though.

It only took a few seconds more to determine that there was nothing of any use in the house; nothing to be learned. Swallowing back a bit of bile as he tried not to imagine the details of what had happened there, Raedrick turned and stepped back outside.

Hiram was on foot, his horse hobbled to the fence, and walking his way down the field, eyes down. Gilroy was just coming out of the shed. He spotted Raedrick and waved him over.

"There's a bedroll and a lantern inside," Gilroy said as Raedrick reached him. His eyebrow rose. "Also a cask of ale and a couple hanks of salted pork."

Raedrick's spirits, driven down by the destruction they had found, rose along with his eyebrows. "So this Simon is making a base of this place; it's not just a spot to do away with Telli."

Gilroy nodded. "Looks that way. If - "

"Constable!" It was Hiram's voice.

Raedrick turned to see the fishing man halfway down the field, on the opposite side from the shed.

"I've got some graves," Hiram said, and he gestured for Raedrick and Gilroy to come over.

There were two of them, only visible in the weeds and grass growth by the markers that someone had put in place there. The markers were nothing special, just planks of wood driven down into the earth, one beside the other, presumably at the head of each grave.

"Hard to tell exactly," Hiram said as Raedrick got near, "and I'm certainly no gravedigger. But I'm guessing these aren't long enough to be adults."

Raedrick eyed him askance for a second, then took a closer look at the ground in front of the markers. And yes, there was a slight bulge in the dirt before each marker, like the earth hadn't been fully packed in atop the bodies. He frowned.

"And have a look at the names."

Raedrick squatted down to take a closer look. Into each marker someone had carved letters. Roughly, as though using a knife that was too small or too dull for the job, or the carver had been in a hurry.

The months had worn the carving down, but the names were still easily visible.

On the left - "Sid."

On the right - "Clarice."

"You've got to be kidding me," Raedrick said as he took the names in, and their import sank in. Hard.

"Looks like someone's been playing you for a fool," Hiram said, and there was iron in his tone.

Raedrick rose from his crouch, frowning hard as he considered what this meant.

That Clarice had a "cousin" named Sid was all that Raedrick needed to rule out coincidence. Clearly they--whoever they really were--had come across this place and taken up the names of the dead farmsteaders. But were they working alone?

Or was Tim Federson pulling their strings?

But that made no sense. Tim was the last thing from a genius manipulator. Was it possible he was being played also? Perhaps Melton hired these two to cause trouble. But then why tarnish his own campaign by involving Frederick?

Raedrick was missing a key piece, somewhere, and it rankled.

"We going to bring her in?" Gilroy asked, and Raedrick shook his head.

"Won't do much good if we don't also get Simon, or Sid, or whoever he is. Near as I can tell she's just been in town working with Helena at the school. He's the one doing the dirty work."

"So you figure she's feeding him information and he's running with it."

Raedrick nodded. "If we take her and he learns about it before we catch up to him, he's gone and we'll never see him again." He turned back to the two fishing men. "We've got to catch them together."

"Or maybe," Hiram said, "we camp out here, just over the hill, and wait for him to come back. After we have him, we can get her whenever we want."

Raedrick considered that for a moment, then shook his head. "We don't know how long he'll be gone. May not be for days. Whatever their real game is, it revolves around the election. This evening is the final question and answer period, and final statements from the candidates. If they plan to cause any more mischief it'll be tonight." He looked up at the sun and took a minute or two to calculate the hour in his head. "I think we use tonight's events to flush them out."

Hiram nodded. A moment later, Gilroy did as well.

They returned to their horses, and Raedrick felt the first bit of true optimism he had in days. It was far past time he took the initiative.

As they rode away from the abandoned farmstead, he was wearing a grim smile.

30

———

PUBLIC SPEAKING

*R*aedrick mounted the stairs up to the grandstand in front of Town Hall and stepped up to the lectern where the candidates would be speaking in just a few moments. Mayor Brimly, who had the floor until calling Raedrick up, stepped back to let him take front and center, but paused for a brief moment to give him a serious look and cock an eyebrow his way.

They had talked about the plan for this evening, and what he was going to say to the crowd. All the same, Brimly always got a bit fidgety when the dice were cast, and no doubt he was feeling it for this one.

Raedrick nodded at him, then took the lectern, laying his hand down atop its edges.

He looked out at the crowd filling the street; almost the entire adult population of Lydelton, minus the fishing men who were out for the evening catch, and a great many from elsewhere in the Vale. There were many faces he didn't know, and no wonder.

He didn't think he'd ever seen a gathering this size in the entire time he'd been in the Vale.

He'd spoken in public enough that the concept didn't frighten him. But all the same, he'd never had to speak to a group this large before.

He cleared his throat to fight down a sudden case of nerves.

Might as well get on with it.

"Good evening," he said in his old parade-ground voice. Back in his Army days, his squad could hear his orders from a hundred yards away; he silently hoped he hadn't lost his touch with it.

In the front row, one of the fishing men in the crowd said, "Hiya, Constable," in reply, and some of the surrounding people chuckled.

Raedrick flashed him a grateful grin. For some reason, that simple greeting caused the butterflies in his stomach to settle.

"Mayor Brimly asked me to fill you in on my investigation of this weeks' events. Since they touch on the election, it's important everyone has the facts as we currently know them." He swept his gaze around until he spied Holb, the tavern-keeper, near the rear of the crowd. Focusing in on him, Raedrick said, "I'll be brief so you can get to the candidates quickly."

"First," he held up his index finger to accentuate his words, "as you know I have Frederick Melton and two of the ranch hands from the Melton Ranch in custody for the killing of Pat Holcomb."

A stirring in the crowd accompanied those words. Some of the fishing men grumbled to each other, and a cluster of Melton men off to the left cast distrusting eyes on the nearest men in grey cloaks to them.

Raedrick hurried before the grumbling became something more.

"The reason they attacked Master Holcomb is that a man delivered a letter to them, forged to look as though it had come from me. They thought they were doing my bidding when they took him captive and later hung him when he tried to escape their custody."

The grumbling ceased, and Raedrick could feel all eyes locking on him intently. Mouths dropped open in shock all throughout the crowd.

"I don't need to tell you that I ordered no such thing." He put on what he hoped was a reassuring smile and paused for a second. Then he held up a second finger.

"Second, you have heard of the allegations young Telli made against Stepan Holiman." Heads bobbed all around, and a number of people cast disparaging looks Stepan's way. "Due to...an incident...Telli delivered her baby early, late last night." He lowered his hand and leaned forward over the lectern. "The baby is clearly the son of a southern man, not Master Holiman."

More shocked faces, and a few gasps.

"I confronted her, and Telli confessed that she had relations with a caravan driver who had been forced to winter over at the McAlister compound, and that the baby is his. She also confessed that a man had paid her to falsely name Master Holiman as the father, to influence the results of this election."

Dead silence throughout the crowd now, and faces were going from shocked to angry.

"From the descriptions the Melton men and Telli gave, the same man was responsible for both events. I am convinced neither Master Melton nor Master Holiman had any knowledge of the man's actions."

"What about Federson?" came a man's voice from somewhere off to the right.

Raedrick shook his head. "Master Federson is as much in the dark as they are, and I have found no evidence of his involvement in any way."

Yet, he didn't say. Though Raedrick couldn't really see Tim as being capable of such acts, he couldn't rule it out completely. He stood the most to gain from Melton and Holiman's collapse.

Still, he wasn't going to accuse him on mere suspicion; if this night went to plan he would have evidence one way or the other soon enough.

"The man who did this appears to be a lowlander. I don't know his true name, but he goes by the name Simon, or Sid." He then described Simon. As he did so, he looked around the crowd, searching.

According to Hiram, who had followed them from the school, Helena and Clarice should be somewhere just left of center-stage...there! They were not immediately next to each other. The press of the crowd had separated them, or Clarice had intentionally distanced herself. There were two fishing men between the two women.

He zeroed in on Helena; her eyes were wide as she recognized the name, and the description.

"I am certain he is not acting alone," Raedrick said. "He delivered the false letter to the Melton Ranch almost immediately after the killing of Lester Goterman three days ago; maybe even before it happened. That means he knew it was going to take place, and someone else who was working with him did the deed." He raised his eyebrows, still focusing completely on Helena. "I believe that accomplice is a woman, and I have a good idea who she is. I expect we will take her into custody soon."

Helena's mouth dropped open and her face went visibly pale, even from a distance. She shook her head in denial.

Raedrick nodded firmly, still locking eyes with her. He held his gaze on her for a long moment, then went back to sweeping the crowd with his eyes.

"That said, I am uncertain of this Simon's whereabouts. So if you see a man matching his description get word to me or my deputies as soon as possible. I don't need to tell you how serious the crimes are that this man and his accomplice committed. Murder. Fraud. And almost worse, the subversion of our election. I promise you, they will not get away with it."

He stopped, took a breath, and nodded again. "Any questions?"

There were dozens of shouted questions, all at once, too many to keep track of, and for a moment Raedrick stood still, trying to figure which to answer first and how.

Then a hand dropped onto his left shoulder and he turned to see Mayor Brimly there. The Mayor gave him that same serious look, but nodding approvingly and applied a bit of pressure on his shoulder, indicating he should step back from the lectern.

Raedrick complied, moving back and to the right to let the Mayor take center stage. He looked back toward Helena, and saw her moving forward, looking around the two men toward where Clarice stood.

Or had stood; the young woman was gone from Raedrick's view now.

Brimly raised both hands and cleared his throat loudly, and amazingly enough the cacophony of questions ceased.

"Thank you, Constable, for the update," Brimly said, turning his head quickly toward Raedrick and nodding to him before he looked back at the crowd. "Now, I know you have a lot of questions, but the Constable needs to get about his work. Please do as he asked and keep an eye out. If he or his assistants ask for help from you, give it. But for right now, we are here to question the candidates about their plans. Please do not ask them about the Constable's investigation. I thought it was important you know what we have learned so far, but the candidates do not know anything more than what the Constable just told you."

He put on his Friendly Mayor grin. "And it's more important

that you learn what you need to from the candidates to make an educated decision between them."

He glanced back at Raedrick again and nodded, and Raedrick took the dismissal for what it was. Turning on his heel, he walked past the seated candidates to the stairs leading down from the side of the reviewing stand.

Melton looked at him with a stern expression; he had been nearly burning with rage when Raedrick had filled them all in on what he had learned. Not at Raedrick, at the circumstances of the plot that had so embroiled his campaign...and his son.

If he got to Simon and Clarice before Raedrick did there wouldn't be a trial. But that was unlikely at this point.

Stepan had been angry as well, but relief and vindication overshadowed that on his face. Raedrick didn't know how things had gone with his wife since they left the Healer's Circle, but he looked much more his former self now.

Tim looked sickly. He clearly knew the crowd would be suspicious of him after these revelations, and had been almost frantic during their earlier meeting to deny any involvement.

Maybe too frantic? It was probably an uncharitable thought...but also not unwarranted.

Now he looked like a man who was steeling himself for an unpleasant time to come, as he faced the crowd's questions.

"Now," Brimly said, "We will commence with the questions and answers. We will go in the order that the candidates made their presentations. Master Melton?"

Melton stood as Raedrick reached the bottom of the stairs. He paid the ranch owner no mind, though, instead turning to look back toward the area of the crowd where Helena and Clarice had been. And sure enough, there was a little surging of bodies from that area.

If she reacted the way Raedrick hoped she was going to, Clarice was now forcing her way out of the crowd, and hopefully would be making a beeline out of town, toward wherever Simon was hiding.

Hiram and Gilroy were stationed on either side of the crowd, at the rear. The nearest of them would follow her at a distance.

It looked like that was going to be Gilroy, so Raedrick hurried over to where Hiram waited. The two of them would circle and link up with Gilroy as soon as they could without giving their presence away, then they would trail Clarice as a group. Once they knew where she was going, they would wait to make sure Simon was also present.

Then they would scoop them both up, nice and easy.

As he rounded the edge of the crowd to link up with Hiram, Raedrick made a silent prayer that it would be so.

31

PURSUIT

*C*larice moved quickly, proceeding down Main Street to the west, and then continuing in the same direction after the paving ended at the final buildings of Lydelton and the road continued as a dirt path running through the grassland toward the edges of the Glamorwood.

The sun was edging below the tops of the mountains to the east, the shadows growing longer, as Raedrick and the two fishing men paused next to the final house on the south side of Main Street's paving stones.

Clarice looked back once, a few hundred paces past the edge of town, and Raedrick resisted the urge to duck for cover. Where they were, near the house's eaves, they would be difficult to spot and anyway it would be very difficult for her to tell who they were.

Dashing about like they were trying to hide from her--especially because they were--would only serve to call attention to themselves.

"Not much out that way," Gilroy said as the young woman's form dipped below the rise of a hill she had been ascending before she looked back.

Raedrick nodded. "Just the old Ranger Station, and then the woods."

"You don't think Simon is hiding out there? I thought the town keeps it locked up."

"We do," he said. "And with a high security lock. But that just means it would take a skilled thief fifteen minutes to pick it instead of five."

He waited to the count of ten, then when Clarice did not reappear, he moved forward at a trot, keeping to the edge of the road so he could hop into the thigh-high grass if she suddenly came back into view.

Behind him, he heard the fishing men puffing as they hurried to keep up.

As he approached the crest of the hill, Raedrick slowed and crouched down. He eased himself forward until he could see over the top to the landscape beyond, then stopped and waved for the fishing men to do the same.

The Ranger Station lay a quarter mile or so ahead and downslope from his current position. Long, with a steep thatched roof that the town paid a pair of local artisans to maintain each year, it was the lone building in view against the green mass of the Glamorwood, which clung to the hills rising into the Saddleback Mountains to the west and north of Lydelton.

The pine forest appeared completely unbroken, untouched by man, but Raedrick knew that to not be the case. Several hunters kept lodges and the like within the forest. Logging parties would foray within a few times a year as well, to obtain materials local craftsmen, or the Covington Brothers, or families would use for construction or firewood. But they picked a different spot for each foray, so it wasn't immediately obvious where they had visited and where they had not.

And probably some folks had less than completely legal

goings-on in the forest as well. Though Raedrick hadn't heard of anything specific, it stood to reason.

Despite, or maybe because of all the human activity that it supported, the forest was always an impressive sight. But right then Raedrick spared it barely a glance, focusing instead on the figure hurrying toward the Ranger Station.

Clarice must have picked up her pace mightily after she passed out of sight of Lydelton; she was most of the way to the Ranger Station already.

Raedrick watched her for a count to thirty, and she did not appear to look back even once. She must have presumed she got away cleanly, since she hadn't seen pursuit in town or on the road.

Big mistake.

He stepped back from the hill's crest and looked back at the fishing men. "She's almost to the Station. Once she's inside we move. Gilroy, circle around the rear of the Station and come around from the west. Hiram and I will go straight in to the door; you'll cover us with your bow. Once we're sure they're both there, we make our move."

"Break down the door?" Hiram sounded almost gleeful at the concept, and Raedrick gave him a look that wiped the growing smile from his face.

"We'll decide once we see what they are going to do." He scooted back up to the top of the hill and peaked over again.

Clarice had reached the Ranger Station, and slowed to a walk. This time she did look back. Then she went to the front door and knocked. A moment later the door opened and she slipped within.

"Ok, let's move," Raedrick said.

He stood and began running downhill toward the Ranger Station.

Right now, Clarice was telling Simon the gig was up, and

they would be formulating a plan to escape.

Or putting their contingency plan, already established, into effect.

He and the fishing men had maybe a couple minutes before they would be leaving on the double. Fortunately there were no windows on the wall of the Ranger Station facing Lydelton, so he had no worry about their being seen until they got to the building.

Still, if they were to spring the trap right, they needed to get there before the couple departed.

And so he ran. Hard.

To his amazement--though it shouldn't have surprised him, really--Hiram caught up and then passed him when they were halfway to the building, and Raedrick shook his head.

Off to the left, Gilroy was going more slowly, as he had to wade his way through the tall grass, so Raedrick slowed up a bit as well, and called, "Slow," to Hiram.

Hiram at first looked amused when he looked back in response to Raedrick's hail, but Raedrick gestured toward where Gilroy was lagging, and after a quick glance Hiram nodded and also pulled back his pace.

Regardless, Gilroy was not yet to the rear of the Station when Raedrick and Hiram reached the nearest wall of the Ranger Station. They paused to catch their breath, and Raedrick looked up at the rising roof peak for a second.

A memory passed through his head for a second, of Julian recounting having to chase the cloak Melanie had made as Raedrick's wedding present--currently hanging from a peg in his and Lani's house--into the Ranger Station after the enchantment she had tried to lay on it went very wrong and it took on a life of its own.

It had slipped into the Ranger Station through a gap in the roof thatching up near where the roof peaked. Raedrick wondered if the maintenance men had fixed that gap during their summer upkeep. If -

"He's almost there," Hiram said, and Raedrick's thoughts whipped back to the present.

Grimacing at himself for losing focus, he looked off to the left and saw that, indeed, Gilroy was about a hundred feet from the rear of the Ranger Station and pushing hard.

It would take him a good minute or two to get around to his station on the west side and unlimber his bow.

Raedrick slipped to the edge of the building and peeked around. Neither Clarice nor Simon were in sight; there was still time to get into position. He looked back at Hiram.

"Let's move. I'll take the far side of the door, you take this side. There are windows, so keep low and out of sight."

Hiram nodded, and Raedrick slipped around the corner, pressing himself against the wall as he went.

The first of the windows in this wall was about fifteen feet ahead. When he was still five feet from the window he stopped and squatted far down into the lowest crouch he could manage, then shuffled forward.

He had to practically duck down onto all fours to keep his head below the window's level.

Then he was past, with just one more window between himself and the door.

The same procedure did for that one, and he straightened fully and made his way to the door. He stopped on this side of it and looked back, to see Hiram crouching to slither beneath the second window.

Nodding in satisfaction, Raedrick stepped across the doorway to get to his position on the other side.

The door swung open, inwards.

"- should have a head start -"

The baritone voice cut off in obvious surprise. The speaker

was a bit shorter than Raedrick, with a round face framed by curly brown hair, and brown eyes.

Simon.

His eyes had gone wide with surprise that mirrored what Raedrick himself felt, but just as quickly they narrowed.

Then a fist struck Raedrick's left cheek and the world spun around him. He felt himself go down onto one knee at the same time as he heard Simon shout, "Run!" To Clarice, presumably.

Raedrick shook his head to regain his bearings and began to push himself up onto his feet. A boot struck his side between his ribs and his hip, and he went down onto his face. Hard.

His world was a wash of pain and shock; he could barely get in a breath.

But he heard the sound of metal drawing against leather clearly. He knew that sound; Simon was unsheathing a blade.

Raedrick needed to move, or he was dead. He tried to push himself up, to roll over, but for some reason he couldn't bring his muscles to do it.

He felt Simon looming over him; sensed the man bending over to grab his ponytail. He'd probably pull his head up by the hair and then slit his -

An impact from above, and then the sound of two bodies hitting the ground off to his right.

Finally, Raedrick's muscles began to respond again, and he shoved himself up onto his elbows to look around.

Hiram and Simon had rolled apart. Hiram was the first back onto his feet, his sword leaving its sheath in a flash of yellow-red from reflected sunset light.

Simon was on his feet a heartbeat later, a long, curved knife in his right hand. It was no sword, but it looked to have a razor edge, and Raedrick would bet a year's pay it was a weapon like that which had gutted Lester.

Hiram advanced, cutting toward Simon's throat as Raedrick

forced himself up onto his knees.

Or tried to. His hip gave a twinge of protest and he had to stop midway.

Simon backed away, letting Hiram's cut whistle harmlessly through the air where he had just been.

Hiram pressed forward with a backhanded cut.

Again Simon danced away.

Raedrick tried again, and managed to get his feet under him.

Hiram advanced again, and again swung his sword.

This time Simon didn't dance backward. He ducked beneath the arc of Hiram's cut and shuffled forward with a grace that made Raedrick's mouth drop open in shocked admiration for a second.

Then Hiram cried out and stumbled forward. His sword fell from hands that went to clutching at his belly. He took another step then collapsed in a heap.

Simon straightened from his attack crouch. The knife in his hand was red along the last third of its length. Raedrick saw a drop pool at the weapon's tip, then fall to the ground.

Gritting his teeth in anger, Raedrick forced himself fully erect and pulled his sword from its sheath. He took a two-handed grasp on the sword's grip, and for a second the engravings on the flat sides of the curved blade seemed to come alive in the reflected sunlight.

Simon grinned at him and flipped his knife into the air, catching it in a backhanded grip before it could hit the ground.

Past him, Clarice had stopped running, if ever she had started. She was clutching at her skirt with both hands as though ready to pull it up to aid in her flight. But from the look of supreme confidence on her face, she didn't think flight would be necessary after all.

Then Simon was rushing straight toward Raedrick. Raedrick darted to the side and cut downward.

Simons changed direction at the last second, rolling in toward Raedrick somehow.

And then Raedrick was off his feet again. Something had struck him in the belly, knocking the wind out of him and sending him sprawling onto his back.

His sword flew from his hands; he heard it skitter off across the ground somewhere off to his left.

To his right, Simon rolled smoothly up into a crouch, his knife coming upward to shoulder-height. There it paused for an instant, then Raedrick tensed as it began its unstoppable journey back down toward his chest.

A flash of regret that he would never see his son...

And then a whistling sound and Simon gave a jerk. He stumbled backward, falling onto his backside, a long, thin shaft of wood protruding from his chest.

Clarice gave a shriek, and Simon looked down at himself in confusion for a second.

Then another whistle and Gilroy's second arrow struck next to the first, right where Simon's heart--if he in fact had one--was.

He dropped onto his back. Raedrick heard a gurgling exhalation and Simon's limbs spasmed once. Then he lay still.

"No!"

Clarice surged across the distance between herself and Simon, all thought of flight apparently gone.

"Noooooooo!" she screamed again, and hurled herself to her knees next to him. She put her hands on his shoulders and shook him, but Raedrick didn't need to examine him to know he was well and truly dead.

He boosted himself up to a sitting position, and Clarice continued to shake him, her cries of denial becoming more ragged with each shake until they became nothing but an unending wail of utmost despair, and she collapsed onto him, weeping onto his still chest.

32

CONFESSIONS

Gilroy led Clarice into the Mayor's office. He walked at her left with a hand on her upper arm, but she offered no resistance.

She was in the same flower-embroidered dress she had been when they had taken her earlier in the evening, and it was torn in places and dirt-stained from her and Simon's attempt at flight. Her hands were shackled in front of her body, and her eyes were downcast, staring only at the floor. Her lush blonde hair, usually done up well in the times Raedrick had seen her in the past, was disheveled, and hung so that it mostly covered her face.

The fishing man guided her to the chair Raedrick had set up in the center of the room, facing the Mayor's desk, and gently had her sit, then he backed away to stand beside the door.

Raedrick, standing at the right-hand corner of the Mayor's desk, looked her over for a moment. She was totally cowed, by all appearances.

On other side of the desk stood the three Mayoral candidates, one and all looking at Clarice with something ranging between contempt and murderous rage. Even Tim.

Especially Tim.

The Mayor was sitting behind his desk, and he looked at Clarice with a more even expression, though Raedrick could see the smoldering fury in his eyes as well.

After a moment, Brimly cleared his throat, and Clarice twitched slightly.

"Young lady, you are facing very serious charges. Murder. Fraud. Election tampering. Assaulting an Officer of the Law." And thank the Gods it was only assault. The cut Simon had given Hiram was not as bad as the cut Lester received, and Master Sebastini had gotten to work on him quickly. Word was Hiram would be fine, in a few weeks. "I understand from the Constable that you desire to make a confession. Is that correct?"

The blonde hair bounced in response to the shallow nod she made. She did not look up.

Brimly glanced at Raedrick and frowned slightly for a moment, then said, "Normally these sorts of things are done in private, before the judge." He gestured to Raedrick's right, where the Judge himself also stood, in his formal red robes with his greying hair in twin braids that hung down to mid-chest from either side of his head. His scribe sat next to the judge at a little desk that had been brought in for this occasion. "But given the circumstances, I want all the parties involved to hear the truth of this matter. Do you still wish to speak?"

Clarice was silent and motionless for a few seconds, then she nodded again, adding, "It don't matter," in a soft voice that was devoid of anything resembling fight or hope; only soul-consuming loss and despair.

The Mayor looked at the judge then, who frowned in thought for a moment, looking at Clarice as though taking her apart with his eyes. Finally, he nodded to the Mayor. "You may proceed."

Brimly gestured to Raedrick, and he put on his Corporal Dressing Down A Bad Private voice. "What is your real name?"

Clarice flinched slightly at the tone, and her head moved upward ever so slightly. When she spoke, it was more loudly, as though she knew clarity was required now. "Norma Elsben."

"And Simon, was that his real name? Who was he?"

"Aye. He was my husband."

Over to the left, Tim flinched visibly, and his cheeks flushed red.

Raedrick continued, "Where do you hail from?"

"All over. We came up from Calas just after the thaw. Figured this would be a good place to stay for a spell, make some coin. Found that old burned out farmstead, and the graves. From what we heard down in the lowlands about the brigand raid here, we figured we could use the names and blend in, and no one would be the wiser. He set up camp there to scout the country and I came to town." Her eyes rose fully now, to meet Raedrick's, and though her expression was still distraught and her tone dead, there was a spark of something in there. "Was easier than I thought."

Raedrick nodded. "You met back up from time to time to compare notes and form a plan, I presume. You've only been working with Helena for a few months; why did you chose her?"

A little shrug of her shoulders. "Old bat, all by herself. Her kind is always a sucker for a sob story."

"You've done this sort of thing before then." It wasn't a question; Raedrick whipped the words at her as a rebuke, but if she took it as such, she showed no sign.

If anything, the corners of her mouth twitched upwards, ever so slightly, as though she was proud of it.

"So tell me if I have this right. You found out the election was coming up. You'd managed to get close to Tim and Lester," he glanced aside toward Tim, whose cheeks were growing even more red. "More Tim, I suppose. Did you convince him to stand for election or was that his idea?"

"Mostly his."

Raedrick nodded. "And Lester?"

She shrugged. "Like I told you the other day. He got it into his head there was more going on between us than there was."

"All by himself?"

She made another small smile, this one sultry, though it didn't touch her eyes. She shook her head. "You know better than that, Constable. A boy like him will cling onto any hint of attention, and expand it in his own imagination. I let him think what he wanted, and play-acted for him that I was more interested in Pat."

"All the while really seducing Tim."

She snorted softly, and shook her head. "Oh I would have, don't get me wrong. It helps reel the mark in. But," she glanced over at Tim and that sultry smile turned mocking, "he was never...up...for the challenge. If you take my meaning."

She raised an eyebrow, and Tim seemed to wither, he shrunk back so bad. He actually took a half-step back into the wall, and lowered his head so as to avoid the eyes of the other men in the room, all of whom had turned to look at him. Melton in open amusement, Stepan in surprise, the Mayor with pity, and the Judge...completely neutral.

For his part, Raedrick had to stop himself from gawking. Fortunately, the parade grounds had taught him to keep his bearing through all manner of distractions.

"But you told Helena you were pregnant, with Tim's child. If you and he never..." He cleared his throat, and left the question unsaid.

"Tim really is a sweetie," she said, in a tone that indicated found that pathetic. "I told him I had been indiscreet with a caravan driver that I would never see again. The fool offered to marry me, and tell everyone it was his." Her dead tone broke as some amusement began showing through now.

"That's what happened to Telli."

Norma nodded. "Simon found out about her situation during his scouting, We decided to use it; it's a great story."

"So you gave Simon one of my bulletins and he wrote the letter for the Melton ranch. Then he went and hired Telli to accuse Stepan, and you got Lester more and more angry with Pat. And once the campaign began, you began to hit the candidates, one by one." He frowned. "How did you get Pat to go down to the lodge?"

"Wasn't hard. Simon slipped a note under his door saying he had dirt on Melton that would take him down, and he would meet Pat there to give it to him."

Raedrick nodded. "So Pat went down to the lodge after finding the note and Simon delivered the forged note to the Melton ranch. You stayed behind here and coaxed Lester into that alley, and stabbed him."

Norma shook her head. "No, Simon did him in. I was with Helena the whole time."

Raedrick blinked; across the desk Melton and Stepan exchanged confused looks with each other.

"That's not possible," Raedrick said. "The Melton hands received the note in the late afternoon that day, maybe even before Lester was killed. He couldn't have done it and gotten there - "

Norma cut him off. "He gave them that note the day before."

Melton's jaw dropped open in shock. "What?"

Norma glanced at him and raised an eyebrow. "He had a couple men on the ranch he paid off, like he did with Telli. He gave them the note, and they did their part."

Melton spluttered for a second. "Kurt? Ramo?"

She shrugged. "Maybe? I didn't ask him their names."

"Were they supposed to kill Pat?"

Another shrug. "We didn't specify. They just had to keep him away until after the election; how was up to them."

Melton closed his mouth and looked over at Raedrick. He didn't need to say what he was thinking; the relief in his eyes said it all. If his two hands were in on the caper, that meant Frederick was at worst a patsy, not to blame for what had happened to Pat at all.

Raedrick was forced to agree, but that wasn't his decision to make, and not the subject at hand.

"Alright. So Simon killed Lester, and your men at the ranch took care of Pat. Then the next day Telli did her part with Stepan." He frowned and looked over at Tim, who was staring at the floorboards, his shoulders slumped and his face red with embarrassment now, instead of the anger that had infused it before. "All this so Tim would win the election?"

Norma nodded.

"Did he know?"

She actually laughed then, mocking laughter, and shook her head. "Of course not."

Mayor Brimly broke in then. "I don't understand. You went to all this trouble...why? To be the power behind the Mayor of a small town in the middle of nowhere, pulling his strings?" From his tone, the entire concept made no sense to him.

Nor did it to Raedrick.

Norma snorted. "You can keep you pissant town. I don't give a whit for it, and neither did Simon."

"Then why?" Brimly asked again.

She leveled a look at him that said he was past daft to throughly stupid. "You've been collecting taxes for years in case the Kingdom comes looking for their money again. Everyone knows about it. All that money locked away somewhere, and only the Mayor knows where, or how to access it."

That wasn't strictly speaking true. The Mayor's staff knew

where the safe holding the tax money was; so did Raedrick and Julian.

But only Brimly knew the combination to the safe's lock. Brimly, and whoever he turned it over to after the election.

Raedrick let out a low whistle. Twisted as Norma and Simon's plan was, he had to admit a grudging respect for its boldness, and for the details they had put in place to make it happen.

All to be undone by a woman going into labor early...

He shook his head and looked across at the Mayor. Brimly looked as though he couldn't believe what he had just heard for a moment, but he quickly got himself under control. Their eyes met.

"Anything else, Constable?" Brimly asked.

Raedrick shook his head. "No, I think that clears it - "

"Are you actually pregnant?" Tim asked, in a pointed, accusing tone. He had raised his eyes from the floorboards and was staring daggers at the woman who he thought until just a few hours ago had loved him. And maybe he actually did love her?

There were tears welling up in his eyes, so maybe so.

Norma looked at him and sneered. Her shackled hands rubbed her belly, and she nodded. "Oh yes. Not yours of course; nor would I have your child even if you were capable of making one." She leaned back in the chair and sighed, looking up at the ceiling. The mockery and twisted pride she had been showing just a moment ago melted from her face. "I'll have that much of Simon still, at least."

There was a world of pain and loss in those last quiet words.

The group sat in silence for a long moment as everyone took in what she had revealed. Finally, Brimly broke the silence with a soft clearing of his throat.

"Well, I think we've heard enough, Constable."

Raedrick nodded, and gestured toward Gilroy. The fishing man came forward and took Norma by her upper arm.

She was still looking up at the ceiling, and gave a little jerk when she felt his touch. But when she looked and saw it was him, and when he gently pulled her upward, she complied, and then followed him as he led her from the room.

"Well," Brimly said as the door latched shut behind them, "that answers that, I suppose. Constable, I'd like you to - "

Melton stepped all over what the Mayor had been about to say, fixing a determined gaze on the judge. "You heard her, judge. Kurt and Ramo were her paid accomplices, doing her bidding. My son had nothing to do with it. He must be released."

Raedrick opened his mouth to reply, but the Judge raised his hand, and Raedrick bit back what he was about to say.

"We only have her word for what those two did," the Judge said. He looked at Raedrick. "From your preliminary report, it appears when Pat tried to escape, the two hands strung him up, and young Frederick approved their actions afterwords?"

Raedrick nodded. "That's my understanding."

"Then find evidence to corroborate Mistress Elsben's account regarding the two hands. After that, we can see to young Frederick."

"Yes, Judge."

It oughtn't be that hard. Separate the two hands and interview them separately. Offer a lighter sentence to the one who confesses first.

"I would suggest an offer of a lighter sentence for the one who confesses first," said the Judge, as though reading his mind, and Raedrick grinned.

"Exactly what I was thinking."

"Very well. Proceed."

"What about her?" Tim's voice was still affronted, and he turned almost accusing eyes on the judge.

The judge shrugged. "I am not empowered to rule on capital cases, even with a confession. She will have to be sent to the Magistrate in Mangin City. But with her confession that is merely a formality. Most likely it will be the gallows for her. After her baby is born and given to an adoptive family, of course."

Tim looked almost about to object; maybe to the time delay. But there was no way to justify taking the child's life as well as hers. Punish the guilty, not the innocent. After a moment's thought he nodded. "Good."

The judge cocked an eyebrow at him then turned back to Raedrick. "Laremy will bring the transcript of her confession to your office tomorrow for her review and signature."

The scribe scowled slightly and gave the judge a sour look-- to his back--but nodded nonetheless. "It may be toward close of business," he said, his tone distinctly deeper than his skinny form would have lead someone to expect.

Mayor Brimly was watching this exchange with a slightly sour expression on his face. "As I was saying," he said in a more forceful tone, "Constable, please prepare a summary of the plot for release to the public. I want to release it by lunchtime tomorrow. If you can get the hands to confess or cooperate by then, well and good; include that detail. If not, save it for later. What's most important is that the people know this plot has been foiled, and that it was not any of the candidates, or anyone else from the Vale, who concocted it."

Raedrick nodded. "Yes, Master Mayor."

It was going to be another late night, looked like.

33

CERTIFICATION

Mayor Brimly scanned the parchment he was holding, his lips turned downward into a frown of concentration and his eyes squinting to make out the writing in the dim lamplight of his office.

He sat at his desk in his shirtsleeves. Raedrick stood in front of him next to a slight man in a blue shirt and brown leggings that were tucked into calf-high boots. He had his collar laced up and wore a serious expression on his youthful face beneath his tussle of dirty blonde hair. A solid wooden chest, bound in iron, sat on the floor at his feet where he had placed it before opening it to give the Mayor the paperwork.

The candidates for Mayor were seated in chairs along the walls--Melton to the left of the Mayor's desk, Holiman and Federson to the right--looking tense as the Mayor read.

And no wonder. Raedrick had escorted the young man from one of the Covington Brothers' warehouse buildings, which the town's election committee had borrowed for use in collating and counting the election votes. It had taken all afternoon and late into the night to finish tabulating the results; it was almost midnight now.

But no one had gone to bed. Even if law and protocol hadn't required informing the Mayor and the candidates of the results immediately, Raedrick was sure nerves alone would have kept them all awake.

The Mayor finished reading and nodded quickly to himself, then placed the parchment down atop his desk and looked up at the young man. "Thank you, Karl. Does the committee have anything else?"

Karl shook his head, and the Mayor nodded a dismissal. The young man turned and left the room quickly. All of the candidates' eyes followed him until he was out, then snapped back to the Mayor.

"Well gentlemen, I think it is safe to say this has been the most...interesting...election to be held in Lydelton that I can recall." That was putting it mildly. "The results have been tallied, and certified by the election committee."

He looked from Federson to Holiman to Melton, and each man stood slightly more erect as the Mayor's eyes met his.

"Congratulations, Mayor-elect Holiman."

Tim blinked, his shoulders slumping for a second. Then he grinned and cuffed Stepan on the shoulder. "Well played," he said in a slightly teasing tone.

Melton stiffened, his eyes narrowing and his lips compressing in obvious anger, and no small amount of disappointment Raedrick was sure. But a second later that was gone, wiped from his face as he put on an expression that could best be called ingratiatingly neutral.

It only made him look more disappointed.

Stepan's mouth dropped open and his eyes widened in surprise. He looked like he couldn't believe what he had heard. When the Mayor stood and walked around his desk to stand in front of him, he still looked flabbergasted. It was only when the two men clasped hands that the spell broke, and Stepan smiled broadly.

Raedrick stepped over and clasped hands with him as well. "Congratulations," he said.

Stepan's grip was a bit less firm than usual. "Thank you, Constable," he said. "For everything." At that last, his grip firmed up and he locked eyes with Raedrick.

He could see a shadow in the man's gaze that said not everything had been set right; and really how could it? He imagined there was probably still tension with Linsy over what had happened, and probably would be for a while, even if subtly. But also there was satisfaction there, and the awed disbelief of a humble man who didn't really expect the accolade he had just been given.

"Just doing my job," Raedrick said, and for a moment it looked like Stepan would say something more.

Then the smith--the Mayor-elect--nodded and released his grip.

Raedrick stepped aside to let Melton approach. The rancher's face was rigidly polite, his "Congratulations" perfectly correct. But his disappointment remained obvious as he clasped hands with his former rival.

Stepan returned the clasp, and surprised Raedrick in his reply.

"For what it's worth, I think some of your ideas are good ones. After I get settled, let's have a discussion about how to start implementing some of them."

Melton blinked, surprised, then nodded. "Of course. I would be happy to." And he sounded a bit less stiffly disappointed than he had a moment before.

"Yes well, time enough for that later," Brimly said. "I think it's time you three called it a night." He looked from Tim to Melton to Raedrick as he said that. "Alas, Stepan, you and I have a few immediate things we have to discuss before bed."

Stepan's smile slipped slightly, but he nodded.

Tim wasted no time in leaving the office. Melton paused only to clasp hands with the Mayor before doing the same. Raedrick followed him out.

As he closed the door behind them, a thought struck him.

"Master Melton."

Melton stopped at the top of the stairs leading down and turned back Raedrick's way, his face guarded.

"Fredrick is comfortable now that he's been released?"

Melton nodded. "None the worse for wear."

"Good." Raedrick had been glad when Kurt took the offer of leniency and flipped on Ramo. Whatever might be said of his father, Frederick Melton hadn't struck Raedrick as a bad fellow. But that wasn't really what he wanted to ask Melton about. "The other day you mentioned you had another matter you wanted to discuss with me."

Melton blinked, then his eyes turned downward for a second, like he was looking back at the memory of their first meeting, seemingly so much longer than a week ago. He shrugged.

"It's moot now. My younger son, Amos, could use some direction. He's restless on the ranch, and I had thought perhaps you might need another assistant. But considering all that's happened..." He shook his head.

It was Raedrick's turn to be surprised. He had heard the rumors about tension between Melton and Frederick, but nothing about any issues with his other son. But thinking on it, he could see how the junior son would potentially become listless or directionless, knowing he was not the primary heir.

With most families it wouldn't be a huge big deal; not all that much to pass down regardless. But with a fortune like Melton had amassed, and more than that, the influence...

Raedrick nodded. "Why don't you bring him by my office next week. We'll have an interview, and I'll see if I can find some work for him."

Melton's guarded demeanor broke, and he smiled the first genuinely grateful smile Raedrick had seen from him. "Thank you Constable," he said, and it sounded like he meant it, and was surprised by it as well. "Good night."

"Good night, Master Melton."

And the rancher clumped down the steps.

34

DINNER DELIVERY

*L*ani and Raedrick were sitting at their table in their home. Steam that carried sumptuous odors rose from the plate Lani had placed in the center of the table-- grilled fish with leeks and steamed beans still in their pods, a loaf of freshly-baked bread, slathered in butter. He had unstop- pered a bottle of wine, from a white vintage down in the plains past Calas, and he took a moment to pour into their goblets; he got a full pour, she a smaller one, just a few sips worth, as she had been mostly abstaining on account of the baby.

They mostly ate at The Oarlock. Made sense, considering it was her family's business and she preferred to help her mother with the dinner load.

But every now and then they took some time to themselves. And after the events of the last week, she had announced at lunch time today that tonight would be one of those nights.

Raedrick did not argue the point.

He grinned at her and raised his glass. She followed suit and they toasted above the feast she had prepared, then she took a shallow sip from hers.

He drank more fully, then half-stood and picked up one of the plates he had set off to the side of the table and began spooning a helping onto it.

"People have been talking about the election results all day," Lani said.

Raedrick nodded. "So I've noticed. What's the sentiment from what you've heard?"

He set the filled plate in front of her and Lani leaned forward slightly--which considering her belly was really all she could manage these days--and inhaled the aromas rising from it. She leaned back then with a contented smile that made the little dimple in her chin pop into focus.

She had always been beautiful, but just then Raedrick considered there was no more lovely sight in the entire world.

"People seem pretty satisfied, from the talk around the common room." She hefted her fork and stabbed one of her bean pods. "Have to say, I'm happy Stepan got the nod instead of Melton."

Raedrick grunted and set to filling his own plate. She cocked an eyebrow at him.

"You don't agree?"

He paused in mid-shovel and looked back up at her. He shrugged. "Melton rubbed me the wrong way, and I am suspicious about some of the goings on down at his ranch in the absence of the law this last year. But I don't think he means any real harm. Some of his plans would help the Vale a lot, if they are fully realized."

Her other eyebrow rose. "But..."

Raedrick finished filling his plate and settled back into his chair. He cut off a piece of the fish and took a bite. The spices hit his tongue hard, a mixture of sweet and salty and hot combining into a whole that was breathtaking.

Literally. The hot was a bit hotter than Lani usually prepared, and he grabbed at his goblet and took another quick drink.

Her smile turned amused, but the question remained in her eyes.

Raedrick sighed and put his fork down. "But part of the reason Julian and I accepted this job is that Glimmer Vale is isolated. No one from the Kingdom really pays any attention to what happens here."

"And you are worried if that changes, you could face trouble."

He nodded. He and Julian were, after all, deserters from the Army.

"But Marshall Leminster knows. You said you and he had come to arrangement."

He nodded again. "But that's just an arrangement between men. Get the lawyers and courtiers involved and who knows what will come of it."

Lani's look of amusement faded, and he could see she was troubled. Then she shrugged and took a bite of her own fish. "Well it's moot since Stepan won."

"Maybe. He told Melton last night he wants to implement some of his ideas. I guess we'll see."

Lani took another sip of her wine and pondered for a moment. Then she shrugged and smiled warmly at him. "Well that's a worry for another time." She reached across the table and laid her hand overtop his. "For now, my gallant husband has once again saved the town." The smile spread to the rest of her face, and her eyes burrowed into his.

Raedrick felt a flush coming, chased onto his face by the warm shiver her touch sent into his hand and up his arm. He shook his head though, and she cocked an eyebrow again.

Seeing the question in her eyes, he shrugged; but was careful not to dislodge his hand from hers. It felt good there.

"I didn't solve the puzzle."

"What do you mean?"

He grinned at her. "You said it yourself: it required a woman's touch. If Linsy hadn't lost her temper and put Telli into labor, we may never have learned the truth of the matter."

Lani blinked, then giggled softly. The giggle became a full on laugh after a second, and she nodded agreement. "Good point." She lifted her hand from his--and he felt a pang of regret over its loss--then wagged her index finger at him. "Let that be a lesson to you, never to discount a woman's wisdom."

He looked at her levelly. Then he laughed as well.

After a moment, Lani pulled herself together and looked back down at the table again. Then she pursed her lips and pushed herself up out of her chair. She gave Raedrick a level look and a teasing smile. "You forgot the water, husband."

He looked over to their small kitchen setup, and the flask of water that still lay on a shelf next to the stove.

"My eternal apologies."

She chuckled and stepped over to the shelf, and reached up for the flask. Then stopped abruptly. She let out a little, "Oh!" and her knees half-buckled for a second.

Raedrick got to his feet in a rush, but she steadied herself with a hand on the shelf. Her other hand went to her belly.

"Oh!" she said more loudly, then turned her head to look at him. Her expression was a mixture of surprise, discomfort, and pleasure all at once.

"Raedrick dear," she said, "I think we need to go to Mistress Kampari."

"What? You mean - ?"

She gave a little shudder, and nodded. Quickly. "Yeah. We need to go to her. Now."

As he moved to gather up the bag of supplies they had set aside for this moment and hustle his wife out of the house, Raedrick reflected that he had never moved so quickly in his entire life.

MESSAGE FROM THE AUTHOR

Thank you for reading my book. I hope you enjoyed reading it as much as I enjoyed writing it.

Every review helps an author out, so whether you loved this book, hated it, or something in between, please take a minute to tell other readers what you thought. All of the online retailers make it very easy to do, and I would really appreciate it.

Feel free to come say hi at my website or on Gab. I always enjoy hearing from readers, especially since you all are, collectively, my boss.

I also have a weekly podcast, Story Time With Michael Kingswood, where I read stories and talk through some of the latest goings on in my world. I'd love to see you there.

Thanks again. My best to you and yours.

Warm Regards,
Michael Kingswood

MAILING LIST

If you enjoyed this book and would like word on new releases and special deals from Michael Kingswood, sign up for his newsletter on his website. Guaranteed to be spam-free, you can opt out at any time. And you can rest assured he will not share your information with anyone, for any reason.

https://michaelkingswood.com/newsletter-signup/

MEMBERSHIP

Michael would like to invite you to become a supporting member of his website. Similar in concept to Patreon, a few dollars a month will give you access to exclusive content, and help him to focus more of his time to writing fun and exciting stories for your enjoyment.

Sign up at his website:

https://www.michaelkingswood.com/membership/join/

ABOUT THE AUTHOR

Michael Kingswood is 20-year veteran of the US Navy submarine force and a lifelong fan of science fiction and fantasy literature. His work has appeared in numerous collections and anthologies, to include the Fiction River Anthology series from WMG publishing. He holds a bachelors degree in Mechanical Engineering as well as a Master of Engineering Management and a Master of Business Administration. He has four children and currently resides in San Diego.

Find Michael Kingswood online at:

www.michaelkingswood.com
www.gab.com/michaelkingswood
rumble.com/michaelkingswood

MORE BOOKS BY MICHAEL KINGSWOOD

Glimmer Vale Chronicles

Glimmer Vale

Out-Dweller

Tollard's Peak

Robbed Blind

The Falconer's Stairs

Campaign Season

Glimmer Vale Chronicles Books 1-3

Stories From Glimmer Vale

Legacy

Hidden Magic

Captive Hearts

Wedding Gifts

Lost Credit

The Pericles Conspiracy

Passing In The Night

The Pericles Conspiracy

Short Fiction

Michael has also published a number of shorter works, links to which can be found on his website.